"You nearly threw away your own life."

Acknowledging defeat, Corrie sat down on the sofa. It was a mistake. Deliberately, Blake sat beside her, and she forced herself to stay still, her heart pounding, yet not with fear.

"You knew I was upset," she muttered.

"A screaming virago is not my idea of a damsel in distress. I respond better to more—" he paused and the gleam dancing in his midnight-dark eyes was a direct challenge "—should I say, more . . . alluring persuasion."

He was smiling. She found her breath had disappeared, and she had to gather her thoughts before she spoke. It was ridiculous, the effect this man was having on her. A tremor rippled through her body, and Corrie knew Blake had noticed it.

She had to be crazy. She didn't even know the man!

Rosalie Henaghan, born and raised in New Zealand, was inspired to write after interviewing Harlequin Romance author Essie Summers on radio. Now Rosalie is the author of many books, whose unique quality stems from her use of events and elements from her own life to enhance her stories. She is convinced that a writer should examine her own background and then, as Essie told her, ''start writing!''

Books by Rosalie Henaghan

WINDSWEPT
Rosalie Henaghan

Harlequin Books

TORONTO • NEW YORK • LONDON
AMSTERDAM • PARIS • SYDNEY • HAMBURG
STOCKHOLM • ATHENS • TOKYO • MILAN

Original hardcover edition published in 1991
by Mills & Boon Limited

ISBN 0-373-03170-X

Harlequin Romance first edition January 1992

I wish to acknowledge the seabirds of the Taiaroa
Heads and the help and inspiration of Shirley
Webb, Warden, and the staff of the Taiaroa
Heads Wildlife Reserve, Otago, New Zealand.

WINDSWEPT

CHAPTER ONE

THE seabird was gliding, his wings a white ribbon against the slate-blue of the evening sky. He dropped, then soared, playing a game with the strong nor'-easterly wind as he crossed the Pacific Ocean, to the headland of the South Island of New Zealand.

From the protection of an outcrop on the clifftop Corrie Seton watched as the northern royal albatross kept approaching, until she could make out his white underbody and the ten-foot wing-span edged with black. Familiar patterns of the seabird's flight towards the isolated Taiaroa headland made Corrie more intent, her hope and excitement rising with each cock-sure demonstration of his mastery of the wind. Without taking her gaze from the magnificence and joy of the bird's flight, she patted the rocky ledge for the binoculars. She swung them up, focusing on the bird's stalky legs and the colour bands.

'Red, red, red! Roddy! It's you!'

Her words were echoed by the joy in her hazel-brown eyes and the flush of colour on her glowing skin. Shoulder-length curly brown hair flicked with red danced with her quick movement of exultant recognition.

The albatross circled above the nursery area of the headland, then turned and glided towards the rocky clifftop where she stood. Within seconds he was flying only four feet above her, allowing the stiff wind to act like a brake to almost hold him in position. His black eyes, set like onyx beads on his pristine white feathered

head surveyed her and a throaty, soft call emitted an
enquiry.

'You remembered, Roddy! Welcome home!' Corrie
answered, trying to keep her voice low despite the rush
of elation. The wind carried him away and she watched
as he flew over the line of the sea around Hidden Bay,
then soared up to the headland where he had been
born eight years earlier. His disappeared briefly beyond
the lighthouse, then flew up again, the late evening sun
shining on him, gilding his white feathers, turning him
into a fairy-tale creature, a bird of magic and myth.
Corrie's hazel eyes widened with the beauty of the
sight, the golden bird backgrounded by the triumphant
red-gold streamers of cloud.

'Roddy, why didn't I bring my camera? That would
have been a shot for the collection!' Corrie murmured
as the albatross, again a creature of black and white,
was hidden by the lighthouse at the headland.

Roddy was the first of the new season's birds to
return to the colony, but others would soon join him.
Corrie's long fingers rapidly adjusted the binoculars to
sweep the sky. Apart from a few shags and some gulls
nearby, the evening sky was clear of any more of the
great birds. She glanced down to her left to Hidden
Bay with its Sea Cottage, the house and private beach
owned by world-famous yachtsman Blake Hanley.
Their next-door neighbour did not live at the property;
he rented it to long-lease tenants, but for more than a
month the place had been empty although her brother
Philip had commented on seeing painters' and builders'
vans at the site. A feather of white smoke issuing from
the lounge chimney told her a tenant had moved in.

Loud cawing and fluttering among the shags nesting
on the opposite cliff of Hidden Bay made Corrie frown.
The area was part of the Taiaroa Heads Wildlife

Reserve and strictly off limits. A former part-time worker at the Centre, Corrie waited for a moment to make sure the birds did not take to the sky, and while they resettled she checked that the seals were still lying like brown slabs on the black rocks below the shag colony. Reassured, she pushed the binoculars back into their case, strapped it into position and zipped up her jacket. With one hand she held her hair and with the other she tugged her hood into place, trapping her hair securely. Prepared, she unfolded herself from the protection of the rocks, the wind striking her face, making her hazel eyes water, buffeting her small frame as she began climbing down the steep hillside to the right to her home, the farmhouse sheltered by its trees and by its own half-moon of beach and cliffs.

Three loud, distinctive cracks from a gun and the alarm cries of gulls and shags were followed by the noise of a thousand wings taking to the skies. Shocked, Corrie lost her footing and, holding on, with her hands tense-knuckled, she moved her feet, toeing the rock until she had a secure hold. Safe, she paused, scarcely able to believe anyone could be shooting in Hidden Bay, possibly at the birds. Her heart jumped as she recalled the poetry of the albatross against the sky, the white underbody a natural target. Roddy! Not Roddy!

She had to stop the shooting!

Sidestepping, half jumping, half running, she took every familiar short cut until she reached the beach. There she hesitated, wondering if it would be better to go home for her car or to use the dangerous but shorter route over the rocks. Cries of birds and their rapid, distressed flight decided her and, turning her back on the farmhouse, she sped across the sand to the corner with its protruding barrier of rocks and sea. Breath spurting, she steadied, knowing she would be

no use to the birds if she fell. If she wasn't already
too late!

The thought of the beautiful albatross being shot was
too awful to contemplate. Roddy, of all the birds! She
had loved him from the moment she had helped to feed
him as an orphan, his baby show of indignation hiding
his real fear. Even the smell and regurgitated look of
the special fish meal the wildlife officer Jenny Anderson
had prepared became acceptable as a means of gaining
the little chick's confidence. And it had worked. Roddy
had come to know and trust them, gabbling noisily
when they trekked up the cliff with his rations, like any
hungry chick to his parents. Corrie's early photographs
of Roddy as a white fluffball chick and as a bumbling,
fat fledgling had marked the start of her career as a
nature photographer.

Waves crashing against the rocks sent spray high in
the air and some drops landed on her cheeks like tears.
Brushing them away, she began climbing the chunky
black rocks, her body agile and her sneakers chosen for
their heavy grip tread. In places she scrambled on all
fours, clawing her way forward, aware of the sucking
hunger of the incoming tide. A pile of stranded bull
kelp from an earlier spring tide separated her from the
last rock. She stretched to her full five feet four inches,
calculated, then jumped. Steadying, she looked along
Hidden Bay.

A tall, black-haired man, his back to her, was
standing immediately below her, the barrel of his rifle
a dark, sinister line pointed to the sand. He was looking
towards the sea, and following the line of his gaze she
saw the truth. A wave carried the dead seabird towards
the bay, his great charcoal-black wings held open in a
last attempt to regain his beloved sky.

Choked with emotion, Corrie launched herself at the

man, knocking him off balance and crashing with him to the sand.

'You murdering monster! You—you—you cretinous heap of carbon! You skinload of scum!' With every tear-filled accusation she hammered her balled fists on the man until she was overcome with her own grief. Beneath her, the man groaned and spat out sand. Black eyes glared at her, then she was seized by his powerful hands and thrown off as he rolled. She sprang upright, but the man stayed on the sand, sitting awkwardly.

'If you've quite finished your barbarous assault you might tell me what I'm supposed to have done.' The clipped harshness of his words matched the angry glitter of his eyes. 'And stop blubbering! I can't abide females who cry!'

'You shot him! Roddy. . .' She could not continue.

'The albatross? You jump too quickly to con-clusions.' His lip twisted at his words, but whether it was appreciation for his own wit or he was writhing in pain as he tried to move Corrie wasn't sure. She hoped it was pain. She hoped she'd broken his arms and his legs and bruised his back. A man who could shoot an albatross and then ask what he had done!

She rubbed her stinging hands, brushing away the clumps of sand, uncaring that most scattered over his face.

'Stop that!'

She stopped. The authority in his voice was total. Angry with herself, with her instinctive response, she looked at the man, and her words died. His movement made her think of a bird with a broken leg, but she bit hard on the impulse to help him, even to pass him the thick stick beside him. She stared at it again. It was not a gun but a walking stick. The man was not the one

who had shot Roddy. She had crash-jumped the wrong
person, and a lame one at that!

'Oh, no! Look, I'm sorry. Here, give me your arm,
I'll help you up. I thought you'd shot. . .' Her babbling
apology was ignored. Leaning on his stick, he levered
himself upright, sweatbeads of pain glistening on his
skin, grey-tinged under its outdoors tan. 'Please, let me
help——'

His silence withered her. She tried again. 'I'm very
sorry.'

'My legs do not affect my hearing.'

Lashed by his sarcasm, Corrie stepped back, realising
that not only had he been surprised and hurt but that
he was furious that she should have pitied his condition.
In dismay at her compounding mistakes, she glanced
along the beach, wondering belatedly if they were in
danger. The sound of a motorbike revving into action
told her the shooter had gone.

Trying not to look at the disabled man's slow walk,
she turned and sat on the rocks. She could not walk
away; she would watch for Roddy until the tide carried
him to land. Her hand brushed against her wet face,
then she pulled out and focused the binoculars, but hot
tears kept fogging the cold glass.

'Sight a little more to your right. The bird had some
control when it landed, but it was definitely wounded.
Probably drowned by now.'

Corrie was surprised the man had spoken, but she
turned her binoculars in the direction he had suggested.
The hope and her sighting of black and white wings
flapping feebly by the point of Hidden Bay came
together.

Roddy was alive!

She had to help the great bird. But how? Philip's
boat? How long would it take her to run back to the

farmhouse, find her brother's keys, unlock the boatshed, check the petrol, launch and start the boat? Twenty minutes, half an hour?

Dismissing the idea, she thought of the runabout the Taiaroa Wildlife Centre used and again calculated the time before deciding it would take even longer to recall staff. Distressed, she trained the glasses out of the Bay's narrow entrance towards the main harbour, hoping to see a small craft. It was useless, the weather was not pleasasnt, the wind was too sharp and the day was losing its battle with the patient night. Another flash of long white underwings increased her anguish. There had to be something she could do!

Roddy was so close.

Could swimming be the solution? Her glance flicked the tall stranger who was struggling to walk across the sand, heading back to the cottage. He could hardly walk, let alone swim. She was the only person with a chance. Studying the sea, noting the tide and wave height, she assessed the possibility. The distance was well within her capability, but her enemy would be the temperature of the water. Hypothermia would attack swiftly. The sea in the area was cold even at the end of summer, but after winter. . .the thought was enough to make her shiver.

Like an answer she saw Roddy hold his wings wide, forcing the wind from the wavetops to lift him, so that for a few seconds he skimmed the crests. Her joy fell as he crash-landed, unable to sustain the movement. Checking his new position, she saw he had flown towards the beach. She could swim to him within minutes.

Dropping the binoculars, she began stripping, kicking off her sneakers and pulling off her jacket and jeans. She hesitated over her light woollen jersey, then

decided to keep it, like her socks, on. It would slow
her, but it would also slow the cold. Tucking it into her
pants, she ran to the sea, pausing to call to the startled
man, 'Get help! Ring the Wild Life Centre!'

'Stop! Stop, you crazy. . .'

The first shock of the water hit her toes, splashed her
ankles and stung her calves and knees. A wave rolled
over her lower body and she gasped at the cold. Above
the wind she could still hear the shouts of the man
telling her to stop. She ignored him and plunged
forward, but ignoring the temperature was an impossibility. The sea was liquid ice on her skin, but she kept
swimming, thinking it would be worth a few minutes'
pain to save Roddy.

The cold was invading her body, stealing her warmth.
Shivers began shaking her, warning her to turn back.
They were one of the first signs of hypothermia, but
she dismissed it. She had known it would be cold and
Roddy could not be far. Concentrating on powering
into the waves, bringing each arm up, out and down,
she pushed through the water. Pain, burning, needling
and piercing, began an agony in her limbs, but she
clung to the thought that at any second she would see
Roddy, the tide would carry him towards her. The ache
in her limbs was a fire reaching to every muscle, and
her chest felt tight. She couldn't feel her hands and her
feet. It was taking her too long. She would have to give
up.

Where was Roddy?

The pain eased. Her legs and arms felt strange, as if
she were being propelled through the ocean by some
battery-operated remote control. Through the glass-
green jagged patterns of the water, she wondered
vaguely if she was in danger, but she was unable to
stop. . .

Choking, spluttering and coughing, her arms flailing wildly, she slowed down; the loss of rhythm was a shock. She trod water, her brain functioning in slow speed as she remembered to wrap her arms around her chest. A wave picked her up and she saw Roddy. It was enough to make her steady and she blinked her eyes clear of the salt water, fighting the tide with her feet so she could intercept the bird.

She was too late.

The right wing struck her and she folded it against the lightly boned body, her numbed hands awkward. Angling the bird, she let the sea carry in his left wing, pinioning him against her chest. She knew she had to return to the beach, but she could not let him go. The cold had won, she would float with Roddy. . .on the dark diamond sea. . .

'Pass him here!'

The words were sharp; she heard them, but they made no sense. Someone prised her arms open and took the bird.

'Look at you! Come on, climb aboard—give me your hand.' She had no strength, so he bent, reached under her arms, and with a sharp lurch of the boat threw her on board. Warm air coursed into her lungs and she struggled as the man held her head and breathed into her mouth again.

'Stop that! You'll have us both overboard!' The order penetrated her dulled perception before the sweet air ran into her lungs. 'Here, put my jacket on. Arm through here, now this one. Pull the hood tight.'

It was strange—she could hear but not follow his instructions, so he had to help her, pushing her arms into place.

'Take the bird. Wrap your arms—here.'

Corrie sat, a rag doll unable to move, rolled in his

jacket, Roddy warm in her arms, her fingers tucked in the feathers. It was too much of an effort to keep her eyes open. . .she was flying, with Roddy, flying above the waves. . .

'Don't flake out on me! Hey—you!' She heard the splish-splash of oars.

'What's your name? Tell me your name!'

She heard him mutter something and the tempo of the oars quickened.

'Come on! Look at me!'

All she wanted to do was sleep, but his persistent questions kept buzzing at her like an annoying mosquito. Resentfully, she struggled to focus on him.

'Good! Tell me your name! Roddy?'

He knew it wasn't Roddy—Roddy was dead. A head wound; it looked so small, barely a red scratch under the feathers. She had been too late. Jenny would take the red bands and the silver Taiaroa identification tag. A jolt jerked her backwards as the boat hit the sand hard.

'Come on, out you get.'

She had to obey him, but she couldn't think how to begin. He lifted her legs and propped her on the edge. Pain began burning her again. What had he done with Roddy?

'I can't carry you! Come on!'

Corrie sat listening. Again he held her and blew him warm breath into her several times. Her head was a block of pain.

'Move it!'

The order jerked her into action. She half fell, half leaned as he lifted, but she was standing.

'Arm around my shoulder. Right? Let's go.'

She flopped against him. It was too hard, too painful.

Why didn't he let her lie on the beach, fly on the beach with. . .? Pain shocked her as he yanked her forward.

'Lift your leg, now the next one. Right!'

He was forcing her to walk, and she struggled against the agonising motion.

'Come on—concentrate! Walk!'

If only he would stop, if only she could lie down. . .

'I'm not letting you give up now! Left, right, left, right. . . Come on, you're not a piece of string. Use your legs. Keep awake!' He was bossy, pushing her upright when she faltered, his voice crisp, scorn for her weakness burning her to keep going. 'Nearly there. . . Quick!'

She fumbled, but he was already wrapping her in a duvet, lying on top of her, his body warm. . .but she was still in her wet clothes. Her chest and abdomen hurt. . .she gagged, her stomach revolting, and the man released her, presenting her with an empty pot plant container just in time.

'Good!' He mopped up her face. 'You'll feel lousy, but you're recovering. Your heartbeat is stronger, and your stomach is obviously starting to function again.'

She was so thirsty. If only he would leave her alone.

'Drink! Open your mouth!' He massaged her throat and jaw and she gulped, her tongue sluggish. Another teaspoon of fluid rolled on it. 'Swallow, blast it!'

She wanted to push the spoon away, but it was easier to make the effort to do as he said: if she obeyed him he might let her sleep and stop yelling orders that kept pulling her back. . . His hand touched her throat and she realised dully that he was feeling for her pulse.

'Getting much stronger. You're going to make it.'

Her thoughts were struggling through layers of cotton wool and when she tried to cut through one thick layer there was still another. The man was always there, wrapping her, holding her. Was she imagining it? She tried to move.

'Good.'

He sounded satisfied. Good? The man was a sadist! Corrie felt wretched. Her head was a fireplace where a giant fire had been lit, scorching its way through her body. She spasmed uncontrollably, her legs and arms peforming some weird catatonic dance. Shivers and tremors raced through her as her muscles flexed and tightened and released.

As the pain lessened, her limbs felt as if they were part of her and not the stray belongings of some unseen puppeteer. Even the pins and needles prickling in her feet and hands became bearable. She experimented with moving her fingers. Soon she would open her eyes, but not yet. . . A shiver ran through her as she remembered the cold sea and she wriggled closer to the warmth, cosseted in a nest of skin. It felt so good, so safe, so protective. The tang of the sea mixed with a male scent and a subtle, spicy cologne teased her into full awareness. Realisation that she was wrapped against a man's firm body made her eyelids fly open.

Surrounded by thick black lashes, deep brown eyes were studying her dispassionately, inches from her face. Instinctively she struggled against his hold. The man from the beach released her and sat up, his hand adjusting the duvet around her shoulders.

'Relax—I'm only holding you to warm you and to stop you hurting yourself. The pain was your body recovering sensation. Have some more of this soup. You'll notice it's barely lukewarm—I couldn't risk diverting any heat from your core.'

There was no fight left in her to either ask questions or avoid the spoon. After several mouthfuls her teeth began chattering and the fluid spilled down her chin and on to the sheet. Ashamed of her own weakness, she was let down by the tears that fell.

'Didn't I tell you I can't stand crying females? It's unfair emotional blackmail!' He was smiling as he mopped her face and she realised he was trying to cheer her. She tried to smile back.

'That's the second beautiful sight of the evening.'

His voice was like the tone of a superb bass; mellow, rich and gentle. Corrie looked at him, startled by the change from the autocrat whose voice had lashed her, demanded her obedience, forced her back, every word hard, crisp and incisive.

'What's your name?'

'Corrie.' It was hard work to shape her name, but he nodded and fed her once more. She felt like a baby bird.

'Just a little more, then I'll let you sleep, Corrie.' She felt his hand slip clinically against her skin and knew he was assessing her temperature. 'Can you move your left hand? Right foot?'

Corrie demonstrated her prowess with difficulty, her limbs awkward.

'Excellent. Now if you'll let me shift out of bed I can let the electric blanket take over.'

He slid out, leaving her feeling bereft, missing the comfort of his body.

'Don't go. . .' she murmured, unable to lift her eyelids.

He left with a quick chuckle, his hand flicking some of her tight curls so she felt them damp on her face. The pillow still smelt of him, warm and comforting. It was good to lie in her haven of warmth, without his constant orders. She was so. . .tired. . .

* * *

A car starting its engine woke her. Befuddled, she rolled over, stretched, then gasped as pain cut the movement. Her fingers touched her ribcage and probed a long, nasty scratch, the source of the sudden pain when she had woken. It seemed strange not to know or remember how it had happened. She felt her skin and realised she was naked. What had happened to her clothes? Where was she?

As she sat up, her chest knifed her and she began coughing. The spasm grew worse, the coughs tearing at her system. She felt ill. Her shoulders struggled high, reaching for air, her whole body fighting for breath.

'Just relax.'

Strong hands held her, then began massaging her back, gradually deepening the pattern of her breathing until the paroxysm finished. Pillows were adjusted behind her and she lay back exhausted, concentrating on the sheer effort of breathing.

'My friend's gone to ring for an ambulance. It will take a while to reach us, so I suggest you try to sleep again.'

His words echoed in her mind. Ambulances meant hospital. Corrie struggled to shift the weight of sheets and blankets.

'Not going,' she panted.

'Don't waste your strength. You should have been there an hour ago, but unfortunately my telephone isn't connected yet.'

'I'm fine,' she wheezed. 'I'll go home.'

'You're a mess.' A frown creased between his deep brown eyes. 'If you tell me your home phone number I'll ask my friend to notify your family. They're probably worrying about you, although they may be used to your crazy behaviour.'

His crisp words stung Corrie, but she was too weak to protest.

'Philip's away,' she coughed. Again the man massaged her back until she could breathe evenly.

'Philip's your husband? No?' His hand picked up her long-fingered white hand. 'No wedding ring. . . The hospital can let your nearest and dearest know. Just so long as no one's out searching for you.'

He left while Corrie fumed, knowing that if she tried to explain that Philip was her brother her lungs would again protest; breathing was difficult enough without risking speech. Her head hurt, and she closed her eyes again to shut out the light, concentrating on the warmth and comfort of the bed. She was sleepy. . .

Men's laughter, rollicking and rich, teased her awake. Corrie lay quiet, listening, but the voices had died to a murmur rising and falling above the sound of the sea. She was at Sea Cottage, but the room was so changed it was barely recognisable. The new tenant must have paid handsomely for the changes, but the result was an artist's dream. Had he changed the kitchen? There would be water there, and she was so thirsty!

The thought gnawed at her and she wondered about getting up. While she lay quiet the pain in her chest was bearable. Would it hurt to move? Easing herself forward, she sat up, then carefully swung her legs over the side of the bed, hitching the shirt she was wearing into place. She paused at the feel of the unfamiliar garments, trying to remember when she had put them on, but was teased with an image of the dark man pulling the shirt over her shoulders. Why hadn't he put her in her own clothes? She dismissed the thought. She had to find water. Her head ached, her chest was a bag of whistling agony each time she moved and she was so thirsty!

The murmur of a distinctive male voice coming from the lounge just along the hall prompted her. She wasn't going to ask or take more help; once on her feet she would be better. A few tentative steps took her to the hall, and she clutched the panelling just in time to stop herself falling. Her backbone and legs seemed to have turned into what Philip called 'custard sandwiches'. The roaring in her head was not from the sea, and she sat on the floor before her body failed, tucking her head between her knees. Gradually her senses cleared and the voices became distinct.

'What a story, you old seadog! Here one night and a bird in your bed!'

'It's true! A Rime of the not so Ancient Mariner! But my bird, as you call her, is more like a half-defrosted chicken, a rather scrawny one, and certainly stupid. Not appealing at all.'

'Pity! I rather like the idea of you being bowled over by a woman of passion!'

'Woman? She jump-tackled me like a trialist for the All-Blacks! And her facility with the more colourful phrases of the vernacular. . .'

Corrie flinched. They were talking and laughing about her! Too weak to stand, she pulled and crawled her way back to the bedroom. 'Stupid!' 'Scrawny!' The words stung. Tears kept forming and trickling past her wet fingers faster than she could wipe them away. What was wrong with her? She hadn't cried in years. . . She had almost reached the bed when she was broken by a spasm of coughing.

'Allow me!'

Corrie felt herself being picked up and placed on to

the bed as gently as if she were a tray of cracked eggs. She lay exhausted, unable to speak.

'He was right—you are a mess!' A pumpkin grin from the blue-eyed man sitting beside her. 'I'm Paul Greywood, pleased to be of service—any time I can put you into bed, just let me know!' He winked. 'First woman I've ever met who knocked a certain friend of mine off his feet!'

'Paul, stop your inanities and give Corrie some water. It's on the shelf above the bed.'

It had to be the only place she hadn't checked. Corrie glanced at the black-haired man leaning against the doorway, his face taut. She wondered how he could have known she was so thirsty, but she drank quickly as the man called Paul held the glass for her.

'Paul, would you go and wait up at the driveway? There's no light and the ambulance might miss the entrance.'

'Corrie, we meet only to be parted!' Paul stood up with a laugh, but he left immediately. There had been no mistaking the authority in her rescuer's voice.

'We disturbed you?' He was examining her with his dark eyes. Corrie remembered his words about a half-thawed, stupid, scrawny chicken and wished she had enough strength to berate him.

'I disturbed you.' She made an effort to speak.

'That's one way of putting it!' A smile lightened his face.

'I. . .'

'Don't talk; save your energy. Your skin's the colour of the walls.'

'Colour co-ordination!' she muttered.

His smile rewarded her effort. A magical smile, it changed his stern, uncompromising, weather-lashed face to a gentle approachability. She could not hold her

anger with him; she was too worn out, and anger
required energy. Even her eyelids felt heavy. When she
opened her eyes the man was leaning against the
doorpost. His stance was that of a man exhausted, his
body stressed with pain. How much had it cost him to
save her? Who was he? What was his name? The sound
of a heavy vehicle made him lift his head and he sighed
with relief.

'The ambulance—I'll open the door. Goodbye,
Corrie.'

She heard the anxious tap of his stick in the hallway
and then the talk of Paul and the ambulance staff, but
her rescuer did not bother to appear. The knowledge
made her feel sad, forlorn and completely rejected.

CHAPTER TWO

CORRIE checked her watch and decided to get up, the sunshine glowing through the windows an encouragement. She wanted to experiment with walking outside. The southerly which had kept her indoors hadn't made her recovery too irksome, but she felt as if she had been cooped up for months instead of days.

Friends had called, but their visits had been limited when they'd discovered how much talking tired her. It was frustrating—she wanted to know all the details of the Wildlife Centre and the extra security measures. The possibility of the shooter returning was a recurrent nightmare. Jenny Anderson, the warden, had discussed patrols and fences, but her visits made Corrie all too aware of the vulnerability of the birds. Roddy was a subject she could not allow herself to mention; she had shut away the memory, promising herself she would examine it up on the wild headland that had been his home. It was still too soon. . .too raw.

Outside, a vociferous greeting from the dogs welcomed her. They followed her around or ran in front and pranced like puppies, stopping their play to gaze at her with anxious, sympathetic eyes when the occasional coughing bout attacked her. In the warmth of the sunshine she took her time walking in the garden, delighting in finding the snowdrops, narcissi, and the fat flower and leaf-buds of spring. An impatient series of bleats alerted her to the demanding presence of two large woolly sheep, last year's pets, confined behind the post and wire fence of the home paddock. Harassed, an unsuccessful horse she had rescued from a pet meat abattoir waited with the patience of eternity, his soft nostrils twitching as he nickered a greeting.

'You're getting fat and lazy, Harry,' she teased, and rubbed his neck as he bent to reach for a tuft of grass growing by the base of the fence post.

'He missed you.' Philip joined her.

'It's been almost two months; six weeks in Australia photographing the wildlife, home two days, then I had my unseasonal swim, three days in hospital and a week stuck inside!'

Together they made their way back to the sheltered patio of the farmhouse.

'I'd like to visit my rescuer today,' Corrie said;

'You know the message Mum and I received from the hospital,' said her brother. 'Paul Greywood is a solicitor and he said he was acting on behalf of his client, who specifically requested privacy.'

'I've got to say thank you—the man did save my life,' she insisted. 'I thought I'd give him the presentation print the publishers had made up for me of the Taiaroa series.'

'Well, it could hardly be more appropriate—photographs taken from Hidden Bay and our beach,' Philip agreed. 'And you do treasure it. . .still, I'm concerned. Why didn't he introduce himself? I think our new neighbour has something to hide.'

Corrie managed a laugh. 'You make him sound like a shady character, and he's not! I know he can be trusted!'

'Wait and see.' Philip checked his watch. 'I'll collect the mail.'

Alone, Corrie sat gazing seawards. She wanted to see her rescuer again. Frowning, she tried to analyse her feelings. She didn't have to close her eyes to remember the man's firm touch; the imprint was with her, flicking at her when she had spare moments. In the past week those times had been frequent. Was it simply a mixture of relief and gratitude? In her weakened state had her emotions been confused? How much of the reactions had been caused by dependence and the forced intimacy of his care for her?

If she saw him in more normal circumstances the attraction might not be present. Almost certainly would not be present, she amended. Standing up, she came to a decision. She would call on him after lunch. At the same time she could return his clothes and collect her jacket, jeans, sneakers and binoculars plus the cute watch she had bought in New York.

His clothes she had washed with interest. The combination had surprised her—the designer shirt made of a luxury lightweight woollen cloth and the trousers, thickly padded and fleecy-lined, the label informing her that they were manufactured for wear in sub-zero temperatures. She had worn a similar pair on a trip photographing penguins at the New Zealand base on the Ross ice-shelf in Antarctica and had also used them on Stewart Island at night, lying in wait for the elusive parrot, the kakapo. She knew how practical, warm and expensive the trousers were. What lifestyle did her rescuer lead? Who would need upmarket clothes one day and specialised climate gear the next?

Her eyes lit with self-mocking laughter as she recalled that her own wardrobe held similar contrasts; the heavy, thermal-lined outdoor garments for bush and mountains, her designer suits for meeting international book distributors and publishers and her everyday casual gear for wearing at the Wildlife Centre and round the farm. But apart from wildlife photographers who else would have such a combination? Explorers? Geologists? Was he a scientist? And why did she have the feeling that she should know him? Had she seen a photograph of her rescuer somewhere? Or was it part of her confused state after her ordeal? Had she imagined he was familiar. . .? It was impossible to recall. She had to see him, if only to stop thinking about the man, and the sooner the better!

Corrie checked her appearance in the mirror. She had taken particular trouble with her make-up and attire. The soft terracotta-coloured blouse gave her pale skin more colour, and her silk scarf in deeper and lighter tones was held in an artistic roll by the hidden clip. Her long-line beige cardigan, which matched her softly tailored trousers, was a conservative combination, but wearing them she looked 'casually elegant', as the designer had promised. She smiled ruefully at the reflection. She appeared confident, but her emotions were see-saws of certainty and uncertainty.

Working with care, she folded the man's trousers and the neatly ironed shirt and placed them in a disposable carrier bag. Her keys jingled as she climbed into her late model four-wheel-drive car. It took only a few minutes to reach the entrance to Hidden Bay, and she turned in to brake sharply at an unexpected barrier. A new gate was locked across the drive, blocking all access. Attached to the gate was a large sign: 'Private property. Alarm system. Trespassers will be prosecuted.'

Amazed, Corrie read the sign twice. She felt as if someone had just delivered her a body blow. No one had sealed off Hidden Bay before. There had never been any need; on the peninsula road there were numerous tourists visiting the area to see Larnach's Castle, Glenfalloch's Gardens, the Taiaroa Wildlife Reserve and the Penguin Place, but few travellers took time to wander down some of the side roads such as the one that led to Hidden Bay and the Beach Farm. Again, she eyed the offensive sign.

Alarm system!

The area was safe. She had never known anything go missing and their doors were seldom locked. The new tenant had rescued her and she owed him some loyalty, but what sort of a man could erect such a notice?

Disgusted and defeated, she pulled out the presentation set with her decorated 'Thank you' note. She was tempted to rip the note up and keep the precious set, but her better nature won, and she slipped the set and the clothes bag into the large letterbox beside the gate. It swallowed the parcels, and as it snapped shut a small light flashed on, indicating the presence of an electronic alarm.

Disbelieving, Corrie stared around her and began to notice other security measures. The old fence had gone, and in its place a new tall one was only partially hidden by the screen of trees, and studying it, she saw the strands which would carry warning of interlopers back to the house. Chilled, she began to believe Philip's laughing assessment. The man had to be hiding something. Yet he had seemed a man of integrity.

She climbed back into her car and swung it towards the farm. Their gate was closed, but it was to keep the stock in the road paddock; her rescuer had no such excuse. She drove the car into the garage and made her way back to the farmhouse, her mood disturbed and disappointed as she admitted how much she had been looking forward to seeing the man. In hospital she had wondered if he would visit, but reasoned that his leg would have made it difficult to drive a car, unless he had the vehicle adapted. When he didn't visit she had made many excuses for him. Once she was home, she had reminded herself that he didn't even know where she lived, unless his lawyer friend had visited him and passed on the information. Since seeing the entrance to Sea Cottage she had known the truth. He did not want to be bothered with neighbours and he intended them to stay away!

With a grim face she began to change her clothes, pulling on familiar jeans and jersey with abrupt, jerky movements. Still upset, she headed towards their own beach, her panacea for problems, until she was halted by the boundary barrier of rocks, dangerous, brittle cinnamon scoria, and the hard greywacke. About to turn, she paused on sighting a peculiar object caught on some rocks and she eyed the necessary route, decided she could reach it without venturing near the finger of arched scoria. Curious, she clambered up the black rocks, but when she recognised her jeans thrown up by the sea she was astounded. Sand-, rock- and sun-bleached, they were still intact and her comb was still in the pocket. Why hadn't the man rescued her gear? What about her watch and her binoculars?

Thinking back, she remembered the man's fatigue. Had he just ignored her gear on the beach? Deciding it served her right? But what about Paul Greywood? He had been likeable and fit. He could have run and collected her clothes and binoculars easily enough. If he knew about them, Corrie reminded herself. Her jeans seemed proof. To lose her jacket and jeans would be bad enough, but the watch and her binoculars. . .

Wasting no time, she began searching the rocks and the pools in case the sea had tossed them on to the same area. Twice her eyes lit hopefully, but each time

she checked, it was just a narrow strand of kelp, not
the leather strap of her binocular case. A sense of being
watched made her look up. Standing at the edge of the
rocks in Hidden Bay was her rescuer. Her anger with
him evaporated, replaced with a surge of joy.

'You appear to have made a good recovery, Corrie,'
he remarked.

Her smile glowed and she had to call on all her
sophistication to stop an inane desire to throw herself
into his arms. His voice held the music she had remembered, the depth and resonance clear against the
murmur of the listening sea.

Rallying, she remembered her earlier mission.

'Yes—no permanent damage, thanks to you. The
doctor said you'd saved him a lot of work. I tried to
call on you to say thank you, but you've sealed off the
road.'

'Unfortunately, I can't block off all access.'

Corrie felt the sting in his words strip away her
pleasure in the meeting. She had been so busy searching for her lost property she hadn't thought about
entering Hidden Bay.

'Why should you? It's such a beautiful little beach,
why not allow others to enjoy it?'

'I prefer privacy to parties.'

She chose not to take umbrage, wondering if he had
sealed the drive because of his sensitivity about his
lameness. His curt hardness could mask a fear of being
pitied by strangers. With a little gentleness and reassurance she was sure he would remove his barriers.
'You're not likely to get many picnicking here,' she
assured him. 'We have occasional trampers and hikers
camping on our beach as it's marked on some maps
and the farmhouse can be seen from the road. That's
how most people find Hidden Bay. Either they explore

these rocks or else they climb to my vantage point with me.'

'On top of the cliff?'

She had to nod as a coughing attack from her long speech caught up with her. Lacking energy, she sat down on a dry rock to recover, but she was aware of his frown.

'You'd better come back and have a drink,' he said. 'I'll ring your brother to collect you.'

'No—Philip's busy. I'll be. . .all right. . .in a. . .minute——' Corrie heaved a gasping breath and closed her mouth firmly in an effort to keep back the cough.

'As you like. I suppose it was too much to hope that you would respect my privacy.'

'Your privacy?' she echoed. 'This area is covered by the Queen's chain. It's public land.'

'To reach here you had to traverse part of my property.'

Corrie looked at the man, trying to keep her anger from exploding. 'I very much doubt that. However, it's possible. I wasn't thinking of you when I was looking for my gear. I found my jeans on the rocks. Why didn't you rescue them?'

'By the time you were fit to leave it was high water.'

Deflated by the simplicity of his answer and its obvious truth, Corrie was silent.

'Each day I've had a look on the beach, but rock climbing is beyond me,' the man went on.

Corrie knew instant shame. She spoke again, but the soft tone was back in her voice.

'Apart from searching the rocks for my gear, I won't intrude again,' she assured him.

His dark eyes studied her and she knew again the thrill of his attraction. 'Come tomorrow—I have your underwear and your jersey, Corrie. Two o'clock? I'll open the road gate, it would be preferable to risking your life on those rocks.'

While she was gasping from the unexpected invitation he turned and walked down the beach, pausing to examine flotsam thrown up by the southerlies. His walk was much easier: the days of cold winds had probably enforced his rest indoors too, making Corrie wonder about the permanence of his disability.

She stood up and began clambering back over the rocks, taking her time, wary of the occasional spray from the returning tide. At the corner she looked back and saw that he was standing by the cottage, apparently looking out to sea. He seemed unaware of her, yet she had the feeling that he had no intention of going indoors until he had seen her off the beach. Annoyed, she jumped down the last few rocks which formed a natural extension of the boundary.

The following day Corrie prepared for her visit, her emotions mixed. As she had told Philip, her rescuer had invited her solely for the purpose of returning the clothes.

'At least find out his name!' Philip slammed the door of her car, and she laughed.

'Third time lucky! If I'm not back by sunset send in the cavalry!'

She turned the key and the motor hummed and caught, singing into action. Experienced in handling vehicles, she backed and turned the car with no regard for her brother's critical gaze, instead waving goodbye with a grin. By the time she drove in through the open gateway to Sea Cottage her expression had faltered. Remembering the previous day, she decided to keep her opinions to herself, and to stay calm and polite.

Yet when she thought of her rescuer she felt as if she was driving straight into the path of a hurricane!

Her first surprise was the entranceway. Previously, the area had been a shabby, sand-scattered, toy-littered yard, but as she pulled up she noted the professional landscaping, the tiled paving, and the new shrubs softening the harsh lines of the garage. Down by the beach the old, drunken lean-to boatshed on the jetty had been straightened up and given respectability with paint. But it was the house itself which impressed.

'You can come in, I don't always bite.'

Embarrassed to be caught staring by the man, Corrie opened her door and jumped down. 'It all looks so different. . .' She broke off under the amused glance of his dark brown-black eyes.

'I should hope so! Considerable effort and money went into landscaping it. But Sea Cottage deserves it, and it was evidently neglected before. The last tenant must have been a lazy slob.'

'Ouch! You're talking about a friend of mine. And she wasn't lazy. Gardening wasn't one of her priorities, that's all.'

'Neither was housework,' he shot back. 'I had to have the whole place redecorated.'

'You're blaming the wrong person. The interior hadn't been re-done the whole time we've lived next door and I don't know for how long before that,' she told him.

'You have a point. But your friend should have taken her furniture with her. The decorators billed me for removing and dumping it.'

'You dumped it? I know it was junk, but it belonged to Blake Hanley.'

'Never—the place was let unfurnished.'

'Perhaps to you, but I know the old stuff was here

earlier. The tenants before Misty Warrender stored it in the boatshed. Misty wasn't too well placed financially, so she retrieved it and spent ages cleaning and painting it. If there's any trouble with the estate agents of Blake Hanley tell them to see my brother and me. We'll tell them they should reimburse you. As for that washing machine. . .' Corrie's eyes hardened as she remembered the struggles Misty had faced with the piles of washing from two toddlers. 'I'd love the chance to tell the agents what I thought of Blake Hanley and his high rent.'

'High rent?' he echoed. 'The place was practically given away on the condition that upkeep was maintained.'

'Well, you're very lucky!' she snapped. 'I know the last tenant paid so much she couldn't afford any upkeep. The owner never cared. He hasn't been near the place. I tried to buy it myself, but the agents said he wasn't interested in selling.' Corrie felt sour, recalling her disappointment.

'Hold it!' The man's voice was frost-crisp. 'You're wrong about the rent, and the furniture, and I had my reasons for not selling.'

'Your reasons?' Corrie looked at the man. Anger was pulsing through him. He couldn't be Blake Hanley! In the photos her memory recalled that Hanley had worn a bushy black beard, but beards could be shaved off. . .but Blake Hanley was able-bodied, a former Olympic champion and then a top yachting professional. But accidents could happen. . .

'I'm Blake Hanley.'

Corrie felt the truth yawn open in front of her like the frightening fissure of an earthquake.

'I think you'd better listen to a few facts.'

His words were authoritative, their quietness emphasising the black anger in his eyes. He turned and led
the way inside, and his slow walk gave Corrie time to
gather the exploded tatters of her thoughts. As he
reached the lounge door he stopped.

'Go on in—I'll be with you in a minute.'

His expression made her think of dry ice, so cold it
burnt.

It was a relief to enter the sunlit room. Always she
had loved the lounge at Sea Cottage with its windows
overlooking the bay—but Blake Hanley had ordered
changes. The small windows had been replaced by a
wall of glass and a large space frame, bringing the
beach and sky into the room. The colour scheme of
sand with touches of blue, black and cinnamon had
been taken from the seascape. A lounge suite in sand-
coloured wool looked comfortable, if a little bare, no
cushions softening its square lines. On the walls the
absence of any pictures matched the austerity of its
owner; the only ornament was a meticulously crafted
sailing ship in a bottle.

Corrie frowned. The room reminded her of an empty
sea-shell, beautiful but lifeless. She couldn't help but
recall Misty's scarf-draped walls, her cane baskets full
of shells, driftwood and seed-heads, her bowls of
flowers and leaves, the twins' toys overflowing from a
cane picnic basket in one corner and the books in piles
near every chair. Entering Misty's lounge had been an
adventure; depending on her whim it would feature a
Persian or Pacific or Country Garden theme, and
frequently an eclectic mix of all three.

Standing by the glass wall, Corrie felt reassured by
the constant slap and roll of the waves on the curving
sand—until Blake Hanley entered the room. His anger
seemed to vibrate between them.

'You will examine these rent books. The last tenant's record is on top.'

There was no possibility of refusing his order. Reluctantly, she took the pile of books and flicked open the first. A glance was sufficient, but she checked just to make sure. The details of the rent, upkeep by the tenant and the unfurnished condition were set out clearly. Her mouth went dry as she read, realising that her accusations were wrong. The figure she had understood Misty paid fortnightly was actually the monthly sum. Too late, she remembered Misty's vague budgeting.

'I don't need to see any more,' she said quietly. 'I was wrong, I owe you an apology. I'm sorry.' She put the books on a table and straightened her shoulders, hoping her ready admission would lighten the blackness of his expression. For some reason it seemed important that he did understand. 'I was told you had inherited it years ago and it had been rented ever since. When my brother was beginning to think of marriage I decided I should move from the farmhouse and try to buy Sea Cottage.'

'Even though it meant evicting your friend and her children?'

Corrie heard his sarcasm and decided she wouldn't tell him Misty Warrender was the woman her brother had wanted to marry. 'Your agents should have told you my offer was conditional on the willing release of the tenancy,' she told him. 'I am still interested in buying Sea Cottage. Naturally, I'll raise my offer to include the cost of your improvements.'

'Forget it,' he said shortly. 'Money can't buy this place.'

'If you should change your mind or if you decide to rent it in the future I hope you'll give me first refusal.'

Corrie felt his stare inspect her as if she was a member of an alien species. It was obvious that Blake Hanley's decisions were seldom questioned. If she hadn't known his gentleness she would have quailed, but her memory was too vivid, allowing her to almost feel his touch as he had eased her back into the nest of his warmth. Remembering, she met his look with a smile.

'Is that such an impertinent question, Mr Hanley? Sea Cottage is a place I've always loved.'

She saw the gradual change to approval in his eyes.

'I'll remember, Corrie.' He wasn't smiling, but his anger had washed away as effectively as a tide clears the beach. He gestured to a chair and moved to the sofa. 'My friends call me Blake,' the olive branch was offered with a magical smile, 'or Taiaroa.'

'Taiaroa?' she echoed. 'The headland here, named after the famous Maori warrior chief?'

He nodded. 'My full name is Blake Taiaroa Hanley. My great-great-grandmother was a cousin of the chief.'

Corrie's eyes widened. 'I'd love to hear more.'

'She married a Cornish sailor, John Hanley, from the whaling station set up further down the Peninsula.'

'I know where it used to be, we pass it on the way into Dunedin.'

'They settled in this bay. It was one of the first land titles registered in the area, and it's been in our family since. My father was very proud to be able to claim a link to the Ngati Mamoe, and so am I. Even if we have to take it back more than a hundred and fifty years!'

'So that's why you couldn't sell Sea Cottage,' Corrie murmured. 'It's part of your heritage, Blake.'

'Not just for that reason. I love it too. I lived here until I was ten. When our family moved north to

Auckland I swore I'd return one day with enough money to live here, and now I can.'

'You've finished racing yachts?'

'No! I'll be back. The accident made a mess of my left leg, but the surgeons patched me up and now I'm convalescing and trying to keep a low profile.'

'So you asked Paul Greywood to fob off my family.'

'Yes. I don't want people to know I'm here. You can't imagine the field day the media would have had with the story of our meeting!'

'But you would have been the hero,' Corrie pointed out. 'What's so bad about that?'

'I don't want my privacy invaded. When I give an interview it's limited to the yachts and the race. Most journalists and photographers respect that, but some want something else, and they don't care who they hurt in the process.'

Corrie heard the anger in his voice and kept silent. His dark eyes looked at her and his mouth twitched in a bitter smile.

'Freelance photographers are the worst,' he added.

She shifted her position and leapt to defend her colleagues, 'They only show the images the camera caught.'

'And they select those images to support the innuendo they want to sell. The more salacious the better price. Sex and scandal sells; international sportsmen are a particularly easy target, and libel suits only result in more publicity.'

He moved, levering himself on to his feet, awkward with emotion, limping to the window, where he stood and gazed at the quiet sea. Corrie could only hope he wouldn't ask what she did for a living!

'I'm a bit paranoid about the Press,' he went on. 'It's history. . .but it has led me to be reticent about my plans. It's one of the reasons I sealed off access to Hidden Bay.'

'Obviously the fewer people who wander down, the less chance of you being recognised,' Corrie admitted. 'But sooner or later people will realise you're here. You can't live without support. What about simple things like food?'

'Paul and a dozen others know I'm here. I'm no hermit! They'll deliver things I need. And each one I could trust.'

'You're lucky with your friends,' she remarked.

'They wouldn't be friends if I couldn't trust them.'

'And now you've had to trust me?'

'Unwillingly.'

He sat down with slow movements on to a hard-backed chair, his injury diverting her quick disappointment.

'I don't think your reason is a valid one, but to you it's important,' she admitted. 'I owe you, so I'll respect your wish, except for informing one person—my brother Philip.'

'Why?' he asked.

'Already Philip thinks you have something to hide. He accepted that I didn't learn your name before, but then he knew our meeting was not exactly conventional.' Corrie couldn't help the smile chuckling in her eyes and was warmed when she saw laughter in his. 'Philip won't tell anyone. He was born discreet. Not like me—I'm inclined to let my tongue get ahead of me at times.'

'I've noticed.'

Corrie decided she deserved his acidity. 'Philip's three years older than me, he's twenty-six and he's always been responsible.'

'I don't have a choice, do I?'

'Look, come for lunch tomorrow and meet Philip,' she said impulsively. 'There's just the two of us at Beach Farm.'

'Are you a good cook?'

He was teasing, and Corrie wondered if he had any idea how sensual his smile was when he relaxed. Was it possible to fall in love with a man from his smile?

'No answer, Corrie? I'll eat before I visit!'

His eyes were on her and she spoke hurriedly before he could read her tumbling thoughts.

'I'm not as bad as you! That soup you force-fed me with tasted like ground cardboard and water!'

'Don't blame my cooking. It was part of a supply of emergency food, vitamins, minerals, proteins and so forth. I just added water.'

'It did the trick, at any rate. I'm grateful you saved my life, Blake.' She said his name, enjoying the sound. It suited him.

'So you said in your note. However, I'm surprised you didn't foresee the danger. As a local you must have known the temperature of the water.'

'There seemed no other way,' she explained. 'I considered hypothermia, but I felt I could reach Roddy and return before I was affected.' She frowned, trying to remember. 'I can't understand why I took so long. I'm a fairly fast swimmer. . .'

'Yes, you are,' Blake admitted. 'But you had no chance in that cold. Your bird moved again, heading away from the beach—I saw it as I went for the dinghy. I was afraid you'd drown before I could reach you.'

'I don't even recall much, except reaching Roddy.' It was hard to say his name.

'The bird saved you,' said Blake. 'He acted like a warm lifejacket.'

'I didn't realise. Thank you for trying to save him. I'm glad you put him in the boat with me.'

'Don't give me any noble motives. As far as I was concerned he was a useful tool to keep in any warmth you still possessed.'

Moisture pricked at the back of her eyes and she got up from the comfort of her chair and went to the window, not wanting him to see her emotion.

'I'm not one of your bleeding hearts, Corrie.' Blake's voice was hard. 'It's a waste of time and frequently endangers others. Your swim was typical.'

His words bit, stinging her. Attack was a means of defence.

'Why didn't you tell me about the boat earlier?' she demanded.

'You ask that? After jumping me? Abusing me?' He was beside her, invading her space, and she found herself moving back until the sofa stopped her progress.

'I thought you had a gun.' Corrie held her ground, but he was head and shoulders taller and intimidating.

'Which only makes your action worse. You should have run to the Wildlife Centre and raised the alarm. As it was, you identified the wrong person and set back my own injuries a few weeks. Thanks to your tackle I may not be able to make the Round the World race! Worst of all, you nearly threw away your own life!'

Acknowledging defeat, she sat down on the sofa. It was a mistake. Deliberately, Blake sat beside her, and she forced herself to stay still, her heart pounding yet not with fear.

'You knew I was upset,' she muttered.

'A screaming virago is not my idea of a damsel in distress. I respond better to more——' he paused and the gleam dancing in his midnight-dark eyes was a direct challenge '—should I say, more. . .alluring persuasion?'

CHAPTER THREE

I'M GLAD I jumped you when I had the chance!' Corrie evaded, scorning the quick challenge. 'You knew Roddy needed help.'

'I decided against it,' he admitted. 'The bird had been shot twice.'

'How could you? He was alive!'

'You're being emotional,' he said calmly. 'That's not a rational way to make a decision.'

Corrie could only look at him.

'We're not talking about a canary in a cage!' he snapped. 'The northern Royal albatross is a wild bird, and a big one at that. The one shot had a ten-foot wing span!'

'They're not aggressive,' she protested. 'The Royal's a gentle, intelligent, sociable bird.'

'That doesn't mean he would have let us near him! I thought we'd cause him more distress by approaching him. It was better to let him die in peace.'

'So you were walking away!'

Corrie felt Blake's eyes appraise her coldly.

'Yes. I was hoping to save the rest of the birds, I was going to the Centre to ring the police—they could have picked the shooter up further along the main road. He was wearing a yellow helmet and a blue denim jacket. His motorbike had a distinctive sound—my guess it was a three-fifty. This is a peninsula,' he reminded her, 'and the entrances back to the city are easily covered.'

'Now the birds are under threat of his return any time,' Corrie spoke her thoughts aloud, 'and it's my fault!' She was appalled by the realisation. Her attempt to save Roddy had allowed the rifleman to escape.

'He may not return, and if he does he may be deterred by the extra patrols, and don't forget the gate and fences I've erected. He won't get close to Hidden Bay beach from my side.'

The last three words alerted Corrie.

'You're saying he could approach from our side?' She thought about it for a moment. 'You're right, of course, but it would mean leaving his motorbike on our beach, or halfway up the cliff. Either way he'd be taking a risk.'

'You'd limit him if you padlocked your road entrance gates,' said Blake. 'He'd have to walk from the road, so he'd probably decide there were easier targets elsewhere.'

'Padlock our gate?' Corrie was stunned.

'Yes, just for a few weeks.'

'While the birds are courting and nesting,' she considered aloud. 'But then there are the chicks. They're even more vulnerable, and it could go on the whole year. The last of the chicks flew only a matter of days before Roddy arrived.'

'I have a spare chain and padlock,' said Blake. 'I'll bring it tomorrow.'

Corrie frowned; the idea appalled her. 'Let me talk to Philip about it.' Deliberately, she looked around the room. 'You've made a dramatic change in here.'

'Is that a polite way of saying you don't approve?' He was smiling. She found her breath had disappeared and she had to gather her thoughts before she spoke. It was ridiculous, the effect the man was having on her.

'The big window is magnificent, but it's the space frame I think is really brilliant,' she said. 'It will give protection and shade in summer and virtually doubles the living area. Yet it fits in with the clean lines of the cottage. And of course the colour scheme is perfect.'

'But the bare walls are too minimalistic?' Blake's dark eyes were flashes of humour. 'Next week most of my personal bits and pieces will be brought down from my Auckland base. In the meantime you decorate the couch rather well.'

'The scrawny, stupid, half-defrosted chicken has defrosted to your satisfaction?' Corrie couldn't resist repeating his insults.

'You were not at your best at the time,' he rejoined, not a whit ruffled. 'Your shoulders are nice and straight, you've good muscle tone, especially on your buttocks and thighs. Must have done a lot of swimming and climbing.' He was dispassionate in his assessment. 'Rather long fingers and toes for the rest of your frame—odd, that. Good skin.'

'Have you finished?' Corrie was outraged.

'Barely started, chicken,' he grinned.

'Don't call me chicken!' she snapped.

'Why not? Those light bones of yours are fragile and birdlike. A sharp-tongued little bird—an oyster-catcher?'

Corrie remembered the invective she had thrown at him and kept silent.

'No, wrong colouring,' he mused. 'Your eyes are sometimes quite green, sometimes brown, they change with the colours you wear and, like the sea, with the light.' He smiled. 'It will have to be a seabird.'

'That rules out chicken,' Corrie informed him tartly. 'And I already have a name, thank you.'

Again his smile teased as he ignored her last remark. 'Does it? Haven't you heard of Mother Carey's chickens? Yes, that's it! A stormy petrel! I knew there was something about you I recognised. Danger and trouble!'

His chuckle became laughter, a deep, rich sound, forcing Corrie's indignation to retreat, but in admitting defeat she turned to him. The movement brought them closer together—accidentally she had invaded his space. Her smile faltered and her senses heightened, her breathing became short and rapid, her heartbeat sped.

The power and sensuality of the man charged her being. She struggled to free herself from his attraction. Opening her eyes wider, she looked at him, wondering if he was aware of her chaotic thoughts. His intelligent, expressive eyes were lingering in their gaze; she could feel his will pulling her towards him, like a magnetic field. Their easy conversation stopped, their eyes communicating. Their silence was like a prelude.

A tremor rippled through her body and Corrie knew Blake had noted it. She could see his pulse ticking under the jawline, his beard line already black-shadowed under the skin, his lips slightly fuller than she had remembered, and close up she could see the lines of humour and pain. Her breath caught at the vivid image of his lips kissing her.

She had to be crazy! She didn't even know the man! Hurriedly she bent to fix her shoes. There was nothing wrong with the laces, but the movement would give her a chance to force her thoughts and emotions back under control. The sexual vibrations were pervading and persuasive. She knew Blake was looking at her, apparently not disturbed by her quick, instinctive retreat. 'My shoelace,' she explained unnecessarily. Was that her voice? Her hair fell forward, shielding her face as the retied the lace. It gave her time and cover to plan a retreat, with a semblance of order and sophistication.

Until Blake stretched out his arm and his hand deftly looped the curl back, round her ear, his fingers echoing the movement, exciting her senses. She had to turn to him, look at him and meet his challenge.

Silent, watchful, waiting.

She had the sudden urge to be naked in front of him. She wanted him to make love to her! The knowledge was reflected in his dark eyes. She was surprised by her own physical need. It was too sudden, too rushed, too urgent to be real. He hadn't kissed her, yet he knew her and she knew him. She could almost feel the imprint of his body and touch, the faint sweat breaking on his chest.

'With my body I thee worship. . .' The words of the marriage service echoed in her mind, making complete and wonderful sense. She had to resist the temptation to actually say the words. Never had she experienced such sensations. She was with him and he with her, yet they were not touching.

'For richer, for poorer, in sickness and in health. . .forsaking all other. . .'

She felt the certainty of conviction. Everything was so right. . . Blake was the man she wanted for her husband. . .and he wanted her. It was in his eyes, midnight-dark with tenderness and desire.

She had to stop.

Closing her eyes, she clenched her fists into tight balls, squeezing her long fingers so hard the nails marked the palms. The quick pain drove away the sensual images, and she stood up, breaking and tearing the cobweb strands of closeness between them.

Corrie didn't know the length of time she stood by the window, shaking, gazing at the repetitive waves lazily caressing the sand of the bay. Although Blake was quiet she could feel his reaction, the physical braking of power, like a racing car back under steady control. When she was able to face him again he began to speak, and his tone held danger.

'You're more dangerous than any storm!' He passed his hand across his face. 'I think we've both just weathered a fifty-knot gale in a dinghy. Are you all right?'

She nodded her head, too shocked by her own reactions to do more. 'Can you take honesty?' His eyes met hers and he answered his own question. 'Yes, you can. Corrie, at the moment I'm not prepared to waste time on commitment to any one person. Making love to you might be a pleasurable activity, but it carries emotions and responsibilities I don't need.'

His harsh words hurt; he had spoken of his needs, not hers. And he was so angry. With sudden knowledge of him Corrie realised his anger was more with himself; he was furious because he had been attracted, he had been unable to resist touching her hair. The gesture had escaped his tight control of his emotions. She understood, his words had said it all, but it left her old and sad. To her, the moment had elements of a spiritual experience, a dedication. . .to Blake it had merely been a quickening of sexual attraction. She watched him lever himself up from the couch, his limp pronounced, but he was moving without his stick.

'I'll get your clothes,' he said.

She moved towards the door, recognising the dismissal. In the hall table her attention was caught by a small photographic print framed in leather. Unable to resist, she picked it up, noting the faded image and the rather scarred leather.

'You're looking at my picture of Taiaroa? I bought it

a few years back. It's been like my goad, spurring me on. It's looking a bit the worse for wear, a few trips across the world's oceans have battered it.' A self-mocking expression shaded Blake's brown eyes. 'Proof that I can be sentimental!' The smile touched his mouth. 'Which reminds me—I haven't said thank you for the present.'

'You liked it?' Corric felt gauche hearing her own question. It was ridiculous how much his approval meant.

'What do you think? It's by the same photographer as my Taiaroa picture. I've hung it on the wall in my bedroom.'

'It'll look right at home there.' Corrie put down the small photo on the table.

'I'd think one was taken right outside the front door,' Blake continued, 'though how the photographer managed to be in the right place at the right time. . .he must have asked the tenants and waited all day for the perfect shot! There's another that I think was taken from Farm Beach. You don't happen to know him?'

Caught out by the question, Corrie hesitated. She pulled a wry face, annoyed that Blake, like so many others, had assumed the photographer to be a man.

'From the look on your face he's not your favourite person! What did he do? Annoy one of your pet seals?' He made a movement as though he was going to put a friendly arm around her shoulder, but instead changed direction. 'Photographers are not my favourite people either. Still, one day I'd like to meet him. . .but not for a few weeks. It was a very thoughtful gift, Corrie.'

Blake held out her peach silk and lace bra and pants. 'Revealing,' he said, unashamed. 'Underneath jeans you wear such frivolous knickers!' His dark eyes were dancing.

Corrie took the lingerie, glad she had not been conscious of their removal at the time.

'The socks went in the rubbish but your wool jersey is OK,' he continued. 'Were you the knitter?'

'No, my mother.'

'She lives in Christchurch? Paul said she'd remarried a couple of years ago.'

'Yes, my father died when I was eighteen. Philip took over the farm then,' Corrie told him.

'And you housekeep for Philip.'

Did she imagine the derogatory note in his voice? He had made an assumption, not asked a question. The telephone rang, interrupting them.

'Yes, it was put on the next day.' Blake acknowledged her unspoken question.

'Answer it,' she said. 'I'm leaving. I'll ask Philip to pick you up tomorrow.'

He ignored its insistent tone, his eyes watchful. 'Do you still want me to come to lunch tomorrow?'

'Seeing you won't bother me,' she announced airily, 'and with Philip to protect your virtue you won't feel threatened!'

She gave him a dazzling, white-toothed smile and waved a one-handed farewell, the clothes tucked safely under her other arm. Her car fired on ignition and she swung it around in one smooth lock. At the end of the drive, the gate shut behind her with an ominous clang. The clock on the car told her she had only been absent twenty minutes, yet she felt as if her whole life had been changed. It was as if she had been on the end of a bungie rope, tossed over a hundred-foot drop, and, seconds before she had been smashed, the elastic rope had bounced her back, pulling her to safety.

Soberly, Corrie drove back to Beach Farm, garaged the car, then wandered down to the beach. The walk on the shore calmed her, allowing her to face the sensual attraction she felt for Blake, his reaction and his swift rejection. She couldn't help but wonder what he would have done if she had given way to her instinct, leaned forward and kissed him. The trail of his fingers on her cheek still lingered. She frowned. She'd read of people falling in love on sight, but she'd never considered it a real possibility. Blake Hanley was not her idea of the man she wanted to love! He was too hard, too arrogant, too opinionated, a cold, disciplined man. Definitely not the gentle, compassionate, caring, sharing man she was looking for as a life companion!

Yet when she had looked into his eyes she had been so certain, so deeply touched. . .

The raucous call of the albatross alerted her and she watched as the great birds flew overhead, the first sky calling to the smaller. They were a joy to watch, each swooping and soaring and circling in a game of 'anything you can do, I can do too'!

Their movements were so closely harmonised that Corrie guessed they were a mature pair, bonded for life. She turned back to the shelter of the farmhouse. The magnetism she had felt with Blake had been a powerful biological urge, but there was more to love than sexual attraction, as the giant petrels overhead had reminded her.

'Blake Hanley?' Philip stopped his fork in mid-air. 'Our neighbour is Blake Hanley? You having me on?'

'Of course not!' said Corrie crossly.

'And you didn't recognise him?'

'I'm not a sports follower!' She spoke with some asperity.

'But Blake Hanley's been on telly, in the papers. . .'

Philip grinned. 'Ignoramus! He must think you're
dumb!'

Corrie pulled a face at his brotherly candour and
made to remove his plate. 'Do you want the rest of
your dinner?' she asked.

'OK!' Philip put the forkful into his mouth, chewed
and swallowed. 'He's probably come home to
convalesce.'

'You knew there'd been an accident?'

'The whole world knew—you didn't?' Corrie felt
Philip's disbelief. 'It was a couple of months back.
Where were you?'

Corrie considered. 'Probably up by Wallaby Island.
I don't remember seeing any newspapers after Cairns.
What happened?'

'His yacht was dismasted—a floating container
crashed into them at night. Any more casserole?'

'Yes, but tell me more about the accident.' She held
the dish until he began to speak.

'It was a race between Osaka and Honolulu—apparently they followed a course along the Koru current
alongside Japan, then curved into the North Pacific
current. They'd swung down towards the Hawaiian
group when the container struck. Smash!' Philip's
hands sketched the scene, then grabbed for the dish
from Corrie's suddenly numb grip. 'Watch it—you
nearly dropped it!' He helped himself, then continued
his description, but Corrie was all too able to see the
near-tragedy. 'Blake was nearly wiped out. He was
flung back, and his leg was fractured. Two others were
hurt as well. One was washed overboard, the other had
major bruising and a broken arm. There's no shelter
on the decks of those racing yachts,' Philip added.

'And?'

'The yacht,' Philip spoke each word carefully as

though to a child, 'was dismasted. That means they had no power, they were struggling to retrieve a man overboard and they had two others who needed medical attention. What you might call a mess. They were lucky no one died.'

'Poor Blake, he must have been in agony,' said Corrie softly.

'It was two days before a Japanese fishing boat found their yacht.'

'Two days!' she exclaimed. 'I thought they had radios and things?'

'And things? Blake Hanley would have had satellite navigation, computers programmed for weather, the yacht, wind speed, the works. He's known for his use of innovative technology.'

'So why didn't the organisers of the race send a plane to pick them up? I must ask him tomorrow—he's coming for lunch.'

'Here? Blake Hanley? Why didn't you tell me?'

Corrie looked at Philip in surprise. Her usually pragmatic brother had actually stopped eating at the mere thought of sharing his table with the yachtsman. 'Can you collect him? I don't know if he has transport, or even if he drives. Probably can't, with his injured leg.' She glanced at Philip. 'He wanted to meet you.'

'Me?' he echoed. 'Blake Hanley wants to meet me?'

Her brother's hero-worship irritated her. 'He's only a man!' she said crossly.

Philip whistled. 'But what a man!'

To that statement Corrie had no answer.

Corrie doubted if Philip would have been more impressed if she had announced she was bringing home the Prime Minister for lunch. Having met more than her share of personalities and dignitaries on her travels,

Corrie had learnt to see past the exploits of the person, but with Blake Hanley the person was overwhelming. During the long, sleepless night she had to keep reminding herself that it was just as well their mutual attraction had been doused. She had far too much character to accept sex without love, and Blake had recognised the fact.

'Right! I'll go and post my letter and pick up Blake on the way back.' Philip fiddled with his keys, betraying his excitement. 'See you in half an hour.'

Twenty-eight minutes later, Corrie checked the time when she heard the sound of the car at the top gate. Finishing her beating, she poured the soufflé into the dish and put it into the oven. The heat flushed her cheeks and she drew several breaths to calm herself, before removing her apron to reveal a pale blue jersey and jeans. In the hall mirror she checked her hair; she had clipped it back from her face in a harsh, revealing style, but at the back it rebelled into a fall of curls. It was a style that suited her, but it also carried a 'touch me not' message for Blake to read. There would be no excuse for him to trail a curl back into place!

The car pulled up beside the patio and Corrie saw Blake step out, smiling at some remark. He gestured towards the beach and she guessed he was remembering earlier visits. Forcing herself back to calm, she chopped a few herbs into the salad before carrying it to the outdoor table. 'Good afternoon, Blake!' she felt her breathing speed, but her voice sounded relaxed.

'Good afternoon, Corrie!' His smile lit fires under her emotions.

'Philip and I thought you'd enjoy the meal outside.' She saw his smile widen. 'Don't worry, we know you're housebroken!'

She read his humorous, unspoken comment and saw

his eyes flash an acknowledgement. Their gazes met and held, and Corrie felt her whole body charge with a sensual excitement. It was an effort to look away. The grass was a brighter green, the sky a deeper blue, the sea alight with diamonds.

'It's just such a glorious day!' She wanted to share her delight with him, and her joy soared when she saw it reflected in his eyes. 'Spring pretending it's summer!'

'Pretence is a luxury of fantasy.' Blake's speech was cordial, but the expression in his dark eyes had changed. He had shut her out as certainly as if he had quietly withdrawn and closed the door.

'What would you like to drink, Blake?' Philip returned carrying a tray of glasses. Bereft, Corrie returned to the kitchen. From the window she could see the two men conversing like old friends. She took a deep breath, reminding herself that he didn't wish to get involved, and picking up a tray of canapés she walked out to the terrace.

'Artistic!' Blake's eyes surveyed the tray, appreciating the work in preparing them. He selected one with a degree of care, and she felt a warm, housewifely glow. She caught up the thought with a shock of recognition. She, the independent career woman, had wanted to please Blake Hanley! That was why she had spent the morning in a dither, worrying about what to wear, what to serve, where to eat and how to arrange the table.

Blake included her in the conversation, but she knew he wasn't accepting her. It was almost as if they were in shade, yet the sun still shone.

Listening to Blake answering Philip's questions about yacht racing, Corrie began to see the sailor's commitment and his enthusiasm and touches of warming humour. His injury was shrugged off with a self-mocking smile, but the cause of the accident saw his eyes darken with righteous anger.

'It's the sort of thing that can happen simply because someone somewhere doesn't do his or her work properly or because it costs! The sea wasn't meant for a dumping ground!'

'You gave a lot of publicity to it. I believe the local regulations are being examined, thanks to your influence,' said Corrie.

'I hope to do a lot more work with marine scientists once my next project is up and running.' His smile was endearing. 'I feel rather passionate about the sea and its creatures!'

'You weren't put off by your accident? Philip told me a little about it yesterday. I can't understand why help took so long to reach you,' Corrie questioned.

'The Pacific is a big ocean,' Blake said wryly. 'And no one knew we were in trouble. Our computer gear was wrecked despite its double housing, and the radio smashed too. We had a hand-held one in the life-raft, so we put over a call with that. The range wasn't very good, but we did reach a Soviet trawler. Unfortunately they put out a call that a tanker was in trouble but still making towards the islands.'

'A tanker?' she queried.

'The yacht was named *Banker* for our sponsor. A mix-up in hearing or translation, but it means the race organisers didn't start looking for us. A missed radio call doesn't necessarily mean a yacht has been lost. Our satellite beam was still shifting, but it was thanks to my back-up team checking it and getting worried about our slow progress that the alarm was raised.' Blake pulled a face. 'I don't mind telling you the Japanese fishing boat that reached us first was the sweetest sight!'

'But by then you'd managed to pump the water out, free the mast, rig up a small sail and were heading for repairs,' Philip reminded him.

'My crew did everything,' he shrugged.

'I saw the telly interview with your watch captain. He said it was you who set the courses and gave the orders.'

'I was still capable of that much.' Blake moved to pass Corrie the canapés. 'Do try one—I can recommend them.'

She had been listening, and caught off guard by his abrupt change, she had to remind herself to be cool. She was glad when his gaze went to her brother.

'How much do you know about yachts?' he asked.

'Nothing!' Philip admitted. 'I use a small runabout for fishing. With an outboard I know where I am!'

Was it her over-sensitive imagination or did she see satisfaction in Blake's eyes? Corrie frowned at the thought.

'And you, Corrie?'

'A friend took me sailing in his trailer-sailer in Lyttleton some years ago. It was fun,' she recalled, standing up. 'I'd better fetch the soufflé, or it will be overcooked.'

The meal passed pleasantly, Corrie admitted as she carried the empty dishes back to the kitchen. Blake's enjoyment of the food had been clear and his story-telling of incidents in some of his voyages had been full of interest and humour, often against himself. Each time she heard his chuckle it seemed to warm her, making it impossible for her to dislike him.

When it was time for him to leave, his farewell was as gracious and as much on the surface as her own. He did not offer his hand and took care not to touch her. Corrie had the sudden feeling that they were skaters unsure of the depth of the ice.

She found she was shaking once she had reached the security of the kitchen, and she sat down for a few minutes to try to make sense of her feelings. The sight of the remains of the meal forced her back into action, but she worked mechanically, without the joy of the morning. Was that just because she had been looking forward to seeing him? What had she expected? Instant devotion? Love wasn't like that!

'I timed that right!' Philip looked around the gleaming benches. 'I stayed on chatting to Blake for a few minutes. He gave me a padlock and chain for our road gate, so I put it on. Here's a key, you'd better put it with your car keys.'

'So you did agree. I don't like the idea.' Corrie picked up the key with reluctance. Why had Blake not asked Philip about it in front of her? Had he avoided the topic realising she was opposed to it? Or was it a coincidence.

'I wouldn't have done it for anyone else,' Philip admitted. 'But how could you turn down a favour for Blake, especially when you know he's doing it for the protection of the birds? He asked us to give it a three-month trial. I couldn't refuse him.'

'It's your property, Philip, but I'd hate to see genuine picnickers and campers stopped from using the beach.'

'I said much the same to Blake, but he pointed out that I could always put a sign on the gate telling people to walk to the farmhouse and apply. We could let their vehicles in and out once we'd checked them over.'

'Possibly.' Corrie could see pitfalls. 'Three months isn't long.'

Philip looked at his watch. 'I'll get changed and get back to the top field while it's fine,' he decided.

Alone, Corrie decided she should begin the final sorting of the photographs of her Chinese expedition. She went into her office and began studying her work, but after an hour she gave up. She found it impossible to make decisions; Blake's face with its shuttered expression kept impinging on her mind.

Taking her jacket, she walked down to the beach, having decided she would use the remainder of the day to search the rocks for her gear. The tide was going out, so she took advantage of the exposed shoreline, and, trying not to allow herself to be distracted by the tiny creatures in the hundred and one rock pools, she examined the area, searching ledges and crannies for any trace. Hesitating before she climbed the rocks into Hidden Bay, she admitted another reason—she wanted to see Blake! It was no good telling herself she had seen him a few hours earlier or that even if they did meet, it would make no difference, he had made it brutally clear he was not interested in a relationship. For all she knew, he was married.

The possibility splashed her like cold spray. She sat on a ledge considering it, picturing his mate, a strong, proud and fearless woman like a Kormlada, the wife of the Viking chief. Such a woman would encourage Blake's racing, accepting his frequent absences as part of the price of his success. She could have her own career, which would explain why she had not yet joined her husband.

The bareness of the lounge at Sea Cottage flicked on to the screen of Corrie's mind. Blake had said '. . .next week most of my personal bits and pieces will be coming down from Auckland.' He hadn't said 'his wife'. Was she just as determined on privacy too? Or had his marriage broken up? Was that the reason he had returned?

Corrie felt sick, fragile. Despite the dying sunshine she was chilled. Her cough returned to savage her and she had to rest until her breathing regained its rhythm. The wait gave her time to rethink the situation.

A man with Blake's forthright attitude would have told her he was married when he first acknowledged the sexual attraction between them. Hadn't he asked her if she could handle honesty? Corrie shivered. Honesty was something she believed in and lived by. The frightening depth of passion in her own nature was new. Did she want to make him change his mind? And could she handle the situation if she succeeded?

CHAPTER FOUR

THE sun had turned the sea to gold; Corrie's search had taken longer than she had realised and she was beginning to doubt its purpose. Even if she found her binoculars their weatherproof case might not have protected them for such a time. In Hidden Bay the beach was deserted, apart from a dozen shags perched on a log buttressing the cliff. Their chimneypot nesting sites were on the opposite bank, the seals' colony.

A starfish, almost hidden in the sandy base of a small rock pool, caught her attention, but she moved on when two crabs decided her fingers were worthy of investigation. An empty paua shell gleamed iridescent blue-green, unable to forget the thousand colours of the sea.

The whirr of the shags' wings made Corrie look up, hoping to see Blake. The beach was empty, apart from the fast disappearing birds. She sat statue-like, knowing that something or someone had disturbed the birds. Had the gunman returned? Would she be able to identify him? Was she herself in danger? If only she had her binoculars!

The movement in the edge of the waves was so slight that she almost missed it. A dark shape not quite three feet long emerged, the head with its black feathers highlighted by a band of sulphur-yellow like a narrow crown. Corrie watched with joy as the small penguin stood up awkwardly and began shuffling forward across the sand, its white front a contrast with the dark blue-green, black sheen of its cloak, its flippers, white-edged on black, puppet-like as it began moving up the beach to the cliff.

Corrie hardly dared breathe, knowing the yellow-eyed penguin was timid of humans. As it laboriously hopped higher its webbed feet left a telltale trail, and Corrie realised that lines of similar prints crossed and recrossed the sand down to the tideline. The world's rarest penguin was roosting or nesting in Hidden Bay!

The penguin had begun climbing the cliff; he was heading towards the small ngaio tree, and Corrie noted the dark shadow beyond it. Was there a cave? The penguin made for it with irritating Sunday driver tactics, stopping many times to preen and check until with a last look around he disappeared behind the tree. A quiet yet distinctive 'Hoi-ho, hoi-hoi-ho' made Corrie's wait worthwhile. There was a second penguin in the cave!

Corrie, her professional instinct aroused, looked for a place to set a hide, and realised that the only flat area would be covered at high water. Above her were two pillar rocks and she knew there was a small ledge between them. Her hands were scratched and one finger was bleeding when she reached the ledge, but she was intent only on checking the outlook, relaxing when the slit between the rocks gave a narrow view of the ngaio-shaded entrance and the penguins' front yard and across to Sea Cottage. At the other end another gap gave sufficient space to put the camera facing the bay in a line with the spot where the penguin had left the water. The rocks would shade the area, but looking round she could see no other possibility. Pain made her yelp as she hit her arm against a needle-like projection. She froze, realising the penguins would be alert for any strange sound. The cry of a black-backed gull sailing past was a welcome intervention, and a few seconds later she heard the soft burbling sounds proving the penguins were not alarmed. Glancing at the sun's position, she made up her mind. If she hurried she could set up the hide ready for use at sunrise.

An hour later she had backpacked in most of her gear. Top-heavy, scrambling up the rocks had been difficult, but she knew returning in the dark of pre-dawn would be worse. She placed the hide cover, matched to the colours of the rocks, with care, holding it in place with small rocks. Inside she set up a flat surface for her two tripods.

As she left she sprayed tiny jets of white paint on a few strategic foot- and hand-holds; in the dark her torch would light up the spots marking a safe route away from the cinnamon scroia and above the high-tide slipperiness of the black rocks. At the boundary she looked back. It was impossible to make out the camou-flage cover hidden by the rocks, and the ten-cent white paint spray looked like gull droppings. Satisfied, she set off back to the farmhouse.

'Corrie, it's you!' Philip yawned. 'I thought I heard someone down here. It's not even daylight!'

'I saw a yellow-eye in Hidden Bay yesterday,' Corrie told him. 'I've got to be in position before dawn.'

'You're crazy!' he exclaimed.

'Probably!'

'I'm going back to bed. It's bad enough having to get up at seven o'clock.' Philip frowned. 'Do you want me to go with you? It's dangerous.'

'Not likely! I'd probably have to rescue you and miss out on the penguin! You'd talk at the wrong time,' she laughed. 'Thanks for the offer, but I've spotted the route and the hide's only big enough for one. I made some tea.'

'You've never succeeded with the hoi-ho before,' Philip reminded her as he moved to reach a cup. 'You've got fantastic shots of the Adelie penguins in the Antarctica, and last spring you did a series on the Fiordland crested penguin and the little blue penguins. The yellow-eyed penguin lives here on the peninsula, and it's the one that's defeated you!'

'I know! But this time. . . I must get moving or I'll be too late.'

As she scrambled over the rocks she tried not to think of the past disappointments. She had checked her textbooks and knew the egg would have been laid only a few days earlier. If there *was* an egg, she reminded herself severely as her foot slipped. Steadying, she checked her white spot and edged out again to reach the hide. Once in place she pulled over the sheet to seal off the top, then screwed the cameras on to the tripods. She flashed her torch around a second time to check for crabs, then switched it off and settled herself for the long vigil.

The wash and roll of the waves was a familiar sound, and as her eyes adjusted she could pick up details of the rocks. The penguin cave remained a black smudge, shaded by the small ngaio tree and rocks. She could only hope the birds had roosted in the cave. She poured out a mug of tea and bit into a sandwich, trying to forget the discomfort of the position. The eastern sky began to look grey rather than blue-black and the rare sea mist curled clammy and chill into the hide, so she was glad of her warm, padded suit. She wished she had worn her Walkman; music would have helped fill the void instead of thoughts of Blake.

Imperceptibly the wind awoke and her peepholes became funnels for the wind, the accompanying eerie whistle not helping her gloomy conviction that the

penguins had abandoned the cave. She stood up and
checked the camera, noting the gradual improvement
in the light. The sea mist began to disperse in ghostly,
tattered shrouds.

Shafts of gold were tipping the eastern horizon and
she watched the sunrise, enthralled. The spectacular
cloud colours of violet, grey flaring orange, pink and
soft peach, apricot to cream, evened and disappeared
into the pallid blue of the new morning. Turning to
check on the penguins, Corrie was surprised to see
lights on at Sea Cottage. She frowned as she wondered
if Blake was always an early riser. Hadn't she said she
would stay away from Hidden Bay once she had
checked the rocks for her gear? She was on Blake's
property and her presence would spoil his privacy.
Later she would call on him and ask permission to use
the area at sunrise, although it would mean explaining
her work. He would have to know her career, he
intended to live at the cottage, and she could reassure
him that her work only imposed on the privacy of
animals and birds, not people. It was fortunate that
one of her first studies of the albatross had meant so
much to him. She could even smile at the thought that
his action in ensuring the privacy of Hidden Bay might
have contributed to the presence of the penguin.

As though to mock her thoughts she heard the
gradually increasing sound of two vehicles on their
access road. Her view was blocked, but the cars slowed
to enter Blake's drive. Evidently he had expected his
early guests and had opened the gate. Headlights
painted broad stripes on to the beach and the two cars
stopped by the old jetty and boatshed.

Puzzled and uneasy, Corrie moved to her camera
and adjusted the telephoto lens. The old jetty had been
wired off years ago as unsafe. Under the powerful lens

the structure came into sharp detail. New concrete piles and freshly stained boards told her the surprising truth: the whole jetty had been repaired!

Hadn't she noticed the improved appearance of the old boatshed when she had visited Blake? At the time she had thought it had been done for cosmetic reasons, but she should have realised Blake would have demolished it if it held no purpose. Why had he restored the jetty and the large boatshed? It must have cost him thousands, yet there seemed little point. They were too far away from the port for it to be useful, and after having sealed off road access it seemed strange that he had opened up the bay to small craft. Perhaps because he was a yachtsman himself? Corrie adjusted her lens again and frowned. The old signs warning 'Danger' were still in place. So why were ten men from the two cars walking along it?

Where was Blake? Was he in trouble? What was going on? Light suddenly illuminated the jetty and boatshed. Corrie watched, relieved when she saw Blake at the end of the boatshed. He looked as if he was instructing one of the men to do something. She had her answer as the man ran to the end of the boatshed and began opening the heavy seaward doors.

Blake and the others went into the boatshed and Corrie heard a motor blast into action and the rattle of the doors. A small boat edged slowly into the bay. Long lines glinted in the early light, and she gasped as a large yacht was towed out of the shed. Clear of the jetty the lights went off, but Corrie was able to see the dim white form of the sails being hoisted, even as the tow lines were dropped and the motorboat was anchored. The man in the boat jumped aboard the yacht as it crept alongside, and Corrie recognised Paul

Greywood as he acknowledged a command from the helmsman. Even from his back, she could tell Blake.

The yacht became a dark, smooth, elongated silhouette gliding through the black water. Corrie switched to the seaward camera and used her zoom lens. The speed of the sleek yacht made the focus blur and she had to continually readjust it. The yacht tacked across the bay, then sailed for the open sea past the Taiaroa headland. Instead of steering to the usual shipping route it veered towards the south before she lost sight of it. The powerboat rocking on the swell and the momentary but unpleasant odour of the motor fumes polluting the fresh air convinced her that the incident had not been a phantom ship and her imagination.

Although she knew little about yachts Corrie recognised the clear decks, the smooth long lines and the enormous mast of one built for racing, function and beauty being one. But why the early morning cruise? Why the secrecy?

Burbling sounds broke her musings. The penguins! Below her, a yellow-eye was returning to the cave and its mate was calling farewells from the water's edge. Corrie reached for her camera, but it was badly out of focus, adjusting the lens, her fingers were slow and clumsy with the cold. Just as she framed the shot the penguin went behind the ngaio tree, leaving her with a dark blur. She turned to the second camera, forgetting the protruding sharp rocks and the softness of her arm. The rock did not pierce the skin, but it still managed to hurt her. Nursing her arm, she bent to the viewfinder and was again frustrated by the need to focus. It took vital seconds to adjust the shot and the bird barrelled into the waves with an exultant joy which was the antithesis of her emotions.

Defeated, her right arm sore, Corrie began to

unscrew the equipment. She could scarcely believe she had wasted her chances. It was the sort of mistake even an amateur would never had made. And it was all her own fault, unless she blamed Blake!

Gulls hurled insults as she scrambled back over the rocks. She stopped for a moment and released her frustration in an imitative, raucous screech. A pair of albatrosses flew towards her, their curiosity aroused, and she laughed at their black-eyed inspection, their beauty restoring her humour.

'If I'd had my binoculars, I wouldn't have needed to adjust the focus!' she called after them. It was a nuisance, but she would have to drive into the city during the day to buy another pair. She jumped from the rocks on to Farm Beach. Sunlight was making silver sheets of the east-facing kitchen window and her brother, she hoped, would have plugged in the kettle. He would enjoy her story of how she had missed the photographs.

A piece of shell wedged under her sneaker and she stopped by some lupins to remove it. Dumping her backpack on a flat rock, she squatted down and examined the tread. Her fingers were too big, so she looked around for a stick. As she did so she saw the yacht spotlit by the rising sun, the sea mist clinging to the protection of the dark cliffs forming a tonal contrast. Right on cue an albatross flew ahead.

Her camera was on top of her knapsack and she forced herself to set it up, using the rock as a tripod, focusing and framing, without giving way to excitement. She knew the pictures she was taking were good! Dimly she remembered a line about a painted ship upon a painted ocean. The yacht tacked and she held her breath, finger hovering until the combination of the silver craft showering crystal spray as it raced to the sunrise and the sea mist-shrouded cliffs was in line. There was no chance for a repeat, the sea mist was already dissipating in the sharp wind and the yacht had tacked again. A spinnaker was released and as the wind bellied its curves, the yacht surged through the sea.

Corrie gasped, sure they would be unable to stop in time to avoid the rocks, but with a shout the spinnaker was dropped and the boat gybed to a line with Hidden Bay. She heard the laughter and whoops of joy of the men on board and hastily altered her lens.

The zoom showed Blake, dark eyes laughing, hair wet with spray, rimes of salt on his face, his whole attitude exuberant. He moved before she had the photo she wanted, but she kept shooting, trying to catch his emotion. One of the other crew came into focus and she recognised the charming smile of Paul Greywood. She took shots of him and of the rest of the crew. Her lupin bush was a perfect hide, allowing her to film unobserved. The yacht sailed towards Hidden Bay and Corrie turned back to the farmhouse. She couldn't wait to develop the film.

'Corrie—lunchtime!' Philip called as he came into the studio. 'You've been shut away all morning. Your penguins pose at the right moment?'

'I didn't get any penguin shots,' Corrie admitted as she hung up an enlargement she had been working on.

'After bigger game!' Philip commented after a glance. 'You took these this morning? Out the front?' He was studying the first prints, quickly sorting through the film. 'Look at that yacht—it's incredible! Look at the mast—it's huge!'

'There's a clearer one of it on the enlargement wall,' she told him.

'These are impressive shots, Corrie.'

'I'm disappointed. I was trying to photograph Blake, but it didn't work.' She shrugged her shoulders. 'He needs something elemental. There's not enough power, not enough passion.' She looked at her latest enlargement. 'That's it! Power and passion! The power of the man challenging the elements: the yacht is perfect, the skill of the man harnessing wind power, but he needs a storm, to reveal his hidden emotions.' Eyes alight, she grabbed a couple of photos. 'Look! He could be anyone, the photos don't reveal the man, and a good portrait should speak to you about the person. He's just a man on a boat in these shots. There's nothing in them to tell you that here is a disciplined, dedicated man who's sailed the world's oceans faster than other men. Nothing tells you he's harder than the rocks yet can be more gentle than the summer sea. . .'

She broke off, aware of Philip's perceptive glance.

'You sound as if you were in love with him!' he teased. 'Yesterday at lunch you were all cool sophistication, the professional career woman, yet here you are surrounded by photos of him. I think my sister is smitten!'

'Rubbish! It's just that he has such an interesting face, all angles and planes,' Corrie protested vigorously. 'I should have stayed with the penguins instead of Blake and his boat! There is one shot I'm pleased about,' she continued to distract her brother from his uncomfortably close hit. 'On the wall behind you.'

She had clipped up a dozen enlargements in sequence, and Philip surveyed the display. 'Technically they're all good,' he murmured. 'The second is the one Misty would like—romantic. Reminds me of a Monet painting; sunrise, dawn light, sea mist and the silver yacht.'

'That's what I thought!' Corrie was delighted. Her

brother's artistic sense was sharp. 'I'm thinking of entering it in the Romance category of the National Guild competition. I have my animal entry ready and I have to go to Dunedin today, in any case.' She saw Philip studying another shot.

'This is one of the best photos you've ever taken. It's fantastic, Corrie!'

Corrie looked at the photo and frowned. 'But Blake's obscured!' she pointed out.

'Forget him! Enter this one in the Action category. It's all movement—makes you feel as if you should wipe the spray from your face!' Philip prised it off the wall and set it up in a frame. 'It's a great shot of a yacht at speed. Look at the curved lines, the angle of the sail, the keel of the boat cutting through the water. . .'

Startled, Corrie looked at the shot analytically. Technically, it was good. Focus, frame, angle and light had combined well.

'You must have liked it,' said Philip. 'You enlarged it.'

Corrie nodded and decided against giving her brother the explanation that she had done so only to see if the blow-up would show Blake more clearly.

Philip picked up the entry form from her desk and added ticks to the Action and Romance categories.

'What have you got to lose?' he remarked.

Corrie laughed. 'My reputation as an animal photographer!'

On reaching the grey solidity of the Post Office in Dunedin, Corrie posted off her entries to the Guild competition. The second envelope she delivered to Paul Greywood's office as a small thank-you for his help in her rescue. It was quite a revealing shot of him against the sails of the yacht; the charm was there in his smile, but his attitude showed readiness. 'It's personal, not business,' Corrie commented as she handed over the envelope to the receptionist.

'Mr Greywood is on holiday for three weeks,' the girl told her.

'There's no hurry. It'll keep till he returns.' As she punched the lift button Corrie wondered if Paul Greywood had taken leave because of the yacht.

She took care and time in selecting a pair of binoculars, but she was thrilled with their advanced power. The sun was setting as she drove back to the peninsula and she realised she would be too late to see the penguin return to the nest. It was some comfort to know that the hide was only suitable for sunrise photographs, but the prospect of another early start set her yawning as she garaged the car.

Six mornings later she clambered over the rocks to her hide. The route, even in the dark, was familiar, and as she settled into position she saw Blake's bedroom lights switch on. She checked her watch, Blake was on time! The dawn yacht would sail soon. With bed-warm fingers she fixed and adjusted her cameras, then settled to wait. The yellow-eyed penguins had proved ridiculously difficult to photograph. Each morning one of the pair would shuffle towards the beach. On the way they would stop, stare and preen. Usually the journey took a long time. Corrie grimaced, remembering the results of her photographs. Not one pleased her. There was a space of a few feet where the penguin was lit by the rising sun. If the bird would stop and preen there she would have a good chance of a well-lit picture. Frustratingly, the birds had stopped just before or just after the stripe of light. The photographs of the birds moving in the light had shown the beauty of their nuptial cloaks, but she had rejected every shot. Soon the birds would begin to look bedraggled as their duty on the nest spoilt their fine feathers.

The sound of two cars arriving warned her to re-position herself. On the second morning she had watched the cave entrance as soon as the vehicles arrived and had been rewarded with the birds' gentle preening and affectionate farewells. She hadn't tried to photograph their charming touching, her light meter had confirmed her knowledge that it would have been a waste of film.

The sound of a motor starting made her look up and she saw the jetty lights and Blake's figure outlined, before reminding herself of the penguins. She didn't have time to think of Blake. She smiled as she saw the birds, the female tidying her mate's feathers and the male, his little yellow eye ringed in pink, preening his mate in return. Their tenderness always enchanted her. It was the female's turn to go to sea, and the male stood tall and trumpeted his farewell before returning to the nest.

Corrie hardly bothered to look up to see the white shape of the yacht sail towards the sea, but its presence startled the little bird and it stopped, uncertain in the stripe of light. Corrie clicked the shutter repeatedly as it raised its head and half turned towards her, then as if to hide its nervousness, it preened a few rebellious feathers into place. Still unsure, it moved forward, stopped again and looked out to sea. The yacht had left only a wake pointing to its passage to the open sea. The bird lifted a narrow flipper and Corrie triggered the shutter. The 'guardsman's salute' was an excellent bonus! Surprising her, the penguin turned and appeared to look directly at her, its movements show-ing fear and agitation. Corrie stopped, wondering if the faint clicks of her camera had disturbed the bird. It

looked further to the side and she realised it had
spotted something else on the rocks. Working steadily,
she set up shot after shot. The bird was perfectly lit,
the sand and sea giving a natural background. If she
had stood directing it, she could not have asked for a
more co-operative model.

A rush of sound as the hide cover was ripped off and
the sting of the cold wind froze her into shocked
rigidity. Above her a dark, masculine shape leaned
down and silently focused a dazzling light on to her
camera. The brightness hurt and she shielded her eyes,
but the sound of the film being removed unlocked her
from her fear. She scrambled up, protesting.

'Please—no! Not the film!'

The exposed film danced and curled in the beam of
the light. Aghast, she thrust her hood back to face the
intruder. 'You black-hearted, imbecilic lugworm!' she
roared. 'Do you know what you've done?'

'Corrie!'

'Blake? It's you!' She stared at him, disbelieving, her
anger wiped out by the discovery. Remembering, she
pointed to the tangle of the film. 'You've just ruined a
project I've spent a lot of time trying to set up!'

'I bet!' Blake reached for her second camera.

'What are you doing?' she demanded. 'That's my
camera!'

'Checking your film. I see you haven't taken any with
this one.' He handed it back to her and she stood
astounded as he examined her camera bag.

'There are no more exposed films there,' she informed
him acidly. 'Only my lenses, filters and spare films. And
you have no right to be going through my things!'

'Don't talk to me about rights!' Blake retorted sav-
agely. 'You happen to be on my property without my
permission. It's called trespassing! Damn it, Corrie,

why didn't you tell me you were a professional photographer?'

'You didn't ask me! You presumed I was a live-in dogsbody for my brother. Women are people too! This is the nineties! A career can be just as essential for a woman as it is for a man.'

'I'm not disputing your right to work, just photography? Sneaking round, spying, selling your secret snapshots like a pimp, to the highest bidder. The fact that people have spent a lot of money and effort working to build and trial one of the world's fastest mono-hull yachts in secrecy means nothing to you. If you had any integrity at all you would have asked for the right to take pictures.'

'You would have refused!' Corrie retorted.

'I would have agreed on condition you waited another five or six weeks,' he corrected.

'An embargo? Until you were ready to unveil it!'

'The yacht contains the latest technology and materials. Months of effort went into the hull alone. I don't know why I'm wasting my breath. . .you're like the rest, you don't care so long as you make a few lousy bucks!'

'And you're not in yachting for money? You turned professional after the Olympics,' Corrie pointed out.

'It's necessary to have money. Yacht racing at its peak is expensive. But the money is only part of it. I make money, but I don't sell my friends, my neighbours, or take advantage of famous people and their activities, real or supposed, the way you and your colleagues do.'

'That's a vile thing to say!' Corrie exclaimed.

'You accuse me of vilification?' Blake's dark eyes were sword-points of fury. 'You happen to be neighbours! I believed we were friends.'

'Friends trust each other!' Corrie spat. 'You didn't even trust Philip! Persuading us to chain and padlock our road gate to keep out shooters! It wasn't the birds you were protecting, it was your bathtub toy!'

'Bathtub toy!' The insult fuelled Blake's anger. 'It is one of the world's greatest yachts! And you knew it! You told me you didn't know a thing about yachting! I believed you! You've taken advantage of the situation to get exclusive pictures. It didn't occur to you to ask me, did it?'

'Of course not! I'm not interested. . .'

'Not interested! How can you say that when you were caught in the act? A film full of shots! A hide specially made to blend with the rocks. Tripods and cushions all ready for a long session!'

'It wasn't there for your precious boat!' Corrie snapped. 'Next you'll be saying I owe you for my life!'

'You do!' he retorted. 'But I'm aware that your type has no conscience.'

'That's unfair!' she protested.

'Is it? You promised me you'd stay out of the bay.'

Corrie didn't know which stung the worse, the whip of his anger or the lash of his disgust. She felt tired and defeated.

'All right. I'll admit I should have asked your permission, but I wasn't there to photograph your yacht,' she told him.

'Don't lie to me, Corrie.' His voice was quiet as though his control had returned with his contempt.

'I'm not lying! I'm a professional nature photographer. I was there to photograph the penguins!' She saw his disbelief. 'I photograph animals, birds and insects for a career!'

'Come off it! You couldn't make a living doing that.'

Corrie heard the tinge of hope in his voice. 'Some

probably say the same about yacht racing,' she pointed out. 'If you're good enough to be in the right spot at the right time you can make it once or twice internationally. To make a living requires discipline and knowledge, as well as skill.' She paused and saw Blake's forehead had creased into a grudging frown of admission. He looked towards the beach. Two gulls were squabbling over a dead fish caught in a lump of seaweed.

'Penguins?' he queried. 'You almost had me convinced.'

'Down by the rocks,' she equivocated, and saw Blake's eyebrows twitch.

'There are no little blue penguins there—I would have heard them. They're the noisiest, smelliest penguins you could have picked. A real nature photographer would have known that!' He paused, his eyes narrowed to diamond points of scorn. 'Allow me to congratulate you on being the most ingenious, scheming liar I've ever had the misfortune to meet!'

CHAPTER FIVE

'AND YOU said I jump to conclusions!' Corrie looked round wildly, but there was no escape. Blake leaned against the upper rock, his position controlling hers. Anger gave her the strength to haul herself up the almost sheer rock to face him.

'Your second name should be Thomas, not Taiaroa!' Corrie exploded. 'If you think I'd get up before dawn to get photos of the little blue penguin, you're daft! I was after the rarest penguin in the world, the yellow-eye!'

'Here? In the Bay?' Blake's voice contained doubt. 'I know there used to be a colony of them further along the Peninsula.'

'There still is. But there's a pair nesting here. I've been watching for the past week trying to get photographs without disturbing them. This morning I managed to get some shots I felt good about, and you exposed the film! There wasn't even one shot of your boat on it!'

'You sound so plausible,' he said slowly.

'But you're still not convinced.' Corrie felt desperate, then memory reminded her of the print Blake had carried around the world. He would know the initials in the corner.

'You've got some of my work. The study on Taiaroa Head and the albatross has my initials. And the set I gave you has it too.'

'S and C intertwined,' Blake recalled.

'C for Corrie and S for Seton.'

76

'Why didn't you tell me before?'

'I tried earlier this week, I called on you twice, but you weren't home. And your opinion of photographers was not encouraging!'

Blake's lips twitched and the skin round his eyes creased into lines. 'It appears I have to apologise again.' Salt water ran from his hair and down his cheek, and mechanically he wiped it away. The rising sun lit him and Corrie saw how wet his jacket and trousers were. He intercepted her glance. 'I found the hide yesterday. This morning we hid the runabout on the seaward side of the yacht and I used it to drop alongside the rocks at Beach Farm so I could double back. I caught a couple of waves.'

'You need to shower and change.' Corrie noticed that the yacht had returned silently back into the bay, its sails flowers of the wind. Blake looked at it, like a lover studying the beloved, unable to resist.

'I have to admit, Corrie, you picked an excellent position. He waved to the men on deck and the yacht altered course to the boatshed. 'Though a dangerous one to reach.'

'The penguin didn't give me a choice. I'd better get back—Philip might start worrying.' She looked at Blake. 'It infuriates me to have to ask for your co-operation, but I really want the yellow-eye on film. I've photographed it before, but never successfully.'

Blake looked at her and began replacing the hide. 'I guess you are a professional!' he admitted. 'The penguins beating pride and my temper! Of course you can work here as often as you need. I'm sorry about your film, Corrie.' He picked up the discarded black curls of the negative with a wry smile. 'If I offer you breakfast will that help?'

'Philip will be sending a search party for me,' Corrie told him.

'You can ring Philip—tell him you're with me.' He reached out his hand, offering peace. Corrie slipped hers into his. The simple contact as they walked to Sea Cottage made her understand the bubbling, ecstatic joy of a skylark's song.

'There's the phone.' Blake pointed to the hall table. 'Maybe you could make the coffee while I shower and change, then I'll make you breakfast.'

Corrie was glad he headed towards the bathroom and was not aware of her fingers trembling so much she could hardly control them to tap the correct numbers. It was little use telling herself to ignore his magnetism, when every cell in her body seemed to be cartwheeling. Somehow she phoned Philip, made the coffee, then, seeing the open pantry and noting eggs, flour and sugar, she decided to surprise Blake by making pancakes.

The thermal suit and the element was increasing her temperature, so she undid most of the fastenings, pushing back the padded sleeves and opening the front as she became more and more uncomfortable. As she flipped the fourth pancake Blake appeared. Eyes alight, his wet hair slicked back, clad in jeans and loosely fitting jersey, he was an aftershave advertisement epitomising healthy, male vigour and vitality.

'Smells great, Corrie! I'm so hungry I'm dangerous.' He reached past her to rip off a piece of pancake that overhung the pan, his smile broadening as he looked at her. Corrie tugged the jacket back into place, trying to look unbothered, but the tiny crinkles around his eyes only creased deeper.

'Only you could look so sexy in one of those suits! But I'm sure you want to take it off. If you must put something on, how about one of my sweatshirts? I'm not so sure about fitting you with trousers, maybe tracksuit ones? Or shorts?'

'Anything would be better than this. I'm developing a heat rash!' She shifted the pan off the element and followed as he led the way back to his bedroom. Shoulders tight with the effort to appear natural, she tried not to notice the crumpled bedlinen, but flash-backs were impinging on her: the resonance of Blake's voice, the black hairs curling on his chest, a small scar on his right shoulder. . . Blake's gentleness as he warmed her in the nest of his body. . . She stopped her thoughts, aware of his eyes as he followed her gaze.

'First too cold, now too hot. . . Maybe next time we'll get lucky!'

The smile lurked in his eyes as he walked through to the dressing-room and after opening a drawer he pulled out a red sweatshirt. Printed down one sleeve was an advertisement in junior navy for a club in Cape Cod.

'It will be a bit large.' He pulled out another drawer and tossed her a pair of luridly colourful shorts. 'My sister gave them to me for Christmas; she has a wacky sense of humour. They shrank in the wash!'

Somehow the thought that he had a sister made the situation much easier, Corrie reflected as Blake whistled his way back to the kitchen. His tune was a blackbird collection of repetitive phrases and variations on the theme, broken by the closing of the automatic door.

Within seconds she was cooler as she stripped, then pulled on the sweatshirt and shorts. There was a slight difficulty in making the shorts stay up, but by tucking the sweatshirt over the top she kept them somewhat precariously in place. Blake had forgotten a belt. After rolling back the sleeves of the top she returned to the kitchen, using one hand to hold the shorts up.

Blake was flipping a pancake, a triumphant grin appearing through his frown of concentration as he settled it safely in the pan. Corrie couldn't stop her own chuckle, and Blake looked up, then viewed her with the oversized gestures of a poseur viewing a masterpiece.

'Magnificent! The draperies—the colour!'

Laughing, Corrie pirouetted like a pantomine clown and then, rescuing the sizzling pancake, held the pan aloft in a victorious torch position. She forgot to hold her shorts. Their sudden slide and her wild clutching as she attempted to settle the pan and grab her shorts at the same time sent Blake into a peal of rich, Falstaffian laughter.

'Don't worry, I've seen everything before, remember!' Blake, his massive shoulders shaking with merriment at her dilemma, took his time in relieving her of the hot pan and its contents. His laughter muted to chuckles, he flipped the pancake on to a plate, squeezed a lemon lightly over the pancake, spooned golden syrup on to its surface, then rolled it up.

'This one is yours, won by a splendid display!'

Corrie stood still holding her shorts tightly in position as Blake advanced, the pancake in his hand. She realised that the large syrup-laden pancake would require both her hands.

'No, you have it, Blake,' she told him.

'Such solicitous care for my welfare!' The light in Blake's eyes danced. 'I've eaten a couple—too much of a temptation. I can recommend them!'

Her appetite died as Blake broke off a bite-sized piece. 'What a pity this is such a large pancake.' His teeth gleamed in a flash of white as his smile widened as he observed her waistband-clutching hands. 'I could feed you, like a baby bird.'

Mouth firmly closed, Corrie stood trying to salvage some dignity. Blake took one of the pieces and held it invitingly by her lips. The smell of lemon, syrup and hot pancake tingled in the back of her nostrils and her mouth watered. She was hungry. His thumb and fore-finger stroked the delicate line of her lips, increasing the pressure to move her lips back. The erotic gesture sent a tremor rippling down her back and a sensual langour into her limbs. Opening her mouth, she accepted the piece, conscious of her own white teeth and the proximity of Blake's fingers. Aware of his dark eyes watching the mouth, she swallowed, scarcely noticing the sharp-sweet taste of the food. The intimacy was too disturbing, she could not allow the process to be repeated. She had to regain control. A chair at the table provided the answer, but moving away from Blake took an effort as though she was going against natural forces. Once seated, she held out her hands and Blake passed over the pancake.

'Coward!' he taunted, his voice deep. 'I'll find you a belt.' It was a relief to be alone for a few moments, there was time to catch her crazy thoughts and persuade herself she had imagined the desire in Blake's eyes. Couldn't she just accept him as a friend? Forget his magnetic sexuality?

Corrie grimaced. Ignoring his sexual attraction was an impossibility. It would be easier to turn night into day.

'They say if you keep something long enough you'll find a use for it!'

Even his voice was a delicious torment. She corrected herself. Especially his voice. . .so indicative of the complexity of the man. His chuckle lilted in her ears,

but it was his rare, true laughter, which had laid siege
to her good intentions and feelings. The size of his
massive chest deepened his voice to a baritone. The
music of it made her feel sensual, fragile and vulnerable
at the same time.

With an effort Corrie picked up the almost empty
bowl and poured the last of the mixture into the pan.
Thinking about Blake and his effect on her had to be
put aside whilst she had a chance.

'I picked out the smallest two,' he announced. 'A
memento of my sister's trip to Disneyland, a child's
Goofy belt, or the plain leather?'

'Definitely Goofy, with these shorts!' Corrie smiled.

'Stand up!' His dark eyes agleam, he refused to give
the belt and walked towards her. Sucking in her breath,
Corrie tried remaining unmoved as with his right hand
Blake began to slot the belt under the guide tags on the
waistband, his left thumb against the fine, sensitive skin
near her navel, his left fingers holding the buckle end.
Corrie moistened her lips, tasting sweet syrup with her
tongue. Frissons of sensuality rioted through her skin
as his thumb countered the pressure as he did up the
belt buckle. Held so near him, she could not pretend
she was unaffected. His apparently friendly gesture had
been a skilfully carried out plan. He had known the
effect his hands would cause, the tightening of her
body, the quick quivers of certain muscles, the invol-
untary gasp for breath.

She tried keeping her eyes and thoughts fixed on the
last golden pancake, but he moved, slipping both his
hands around her waist and turning her around so she
was again facing him. The tension between them forced
her to look up, admitting her own need. Blake's eyes,
the laughter gone from them, his irises night-dark, read
her desire.

'Corrie, Corrie! My little stormy petrel!'

His voice was a brown velvet murmur tripping the nerve-ends of her earlobe as he brushed it with his mouth. With a gentleness that set up an aching void he covered her lips with his own, pressing, touching, deepening the exquisite sensation as the tremors of response rippled and shivered through her body.

Like a river dropping to form a waterfall, Corrie felt herself swept away by Blake's touch into a world of crystal, the magic lighting a thousand glowing rainbows as they kissed. Winding her arms around him, she could hear the increasing beat of his heart, enjoy the immense tactile pleasure of running her fingers through his thick dark hair still damp from the shower, see the sculptured mouth descend to meet her own. Their bodies were so close the buckle of his belt imprinted itself on her; she could feel the line of his shirt buttons, the pressure of his hip and thick thigh muscles constrained by his jeans and her own hips. Still the kiss went on, exploring the soft, warm tissues, becoming bolder, insistent, demanding recognition and surrender. When Blake lifted his mouth, all she could do was murmur his name and lean, ragdoll-like, against him.

Nuzzling her earlobe again, his breathing sending wisps of her hair against the sensitive line of her jaw, Blake reached across the smooth surface of her back for her bra fastening.

'Corrie, you're all. . .'

No waterfall had hit with a greater crash. Abandoned, Corrie staggered, drunk with passion. Her thoughts clearing, she saw the flames in the pan, the element red-hot. Blake moved to pick up the heavy lid and put it over the pan, instantly blanketing the flames. Corrie reached out and flicked the master switch off, then looked at the man beside her.

'Thanks, Corrie, it should be safe now. I'll just let it cool. I'll make a note to get smoke alarms—until now I hadn't realised they weren't installed.' Blake smiled and reached for her again. 'You're a passionate creature, my Corrie, you should wear a sign saying "Danger—approach with caution!" You set me on fire!' His low voice was a sweet torment, but Corrie moved to the other side of the table, by the window, setting a distance between them.

'No, Blake!'

He looked at her, one eyebrow raising slightly.

'I might be naïve, but I know that if I kiss you again I'll want you to make love to me.' She paused to gather strength, looking at him, knowing his answer before she spoke but hoping for a different one. 'You once asked if I could take honesty. But can you be honest? Would it just be a sexual encounter for you?'

'You want me to swear undying love? I told you, Corrie, I have other priorities. But we're both responsible adults, we could enjoy each other for a brief time.'

'Like two flies copulating on a window and buzzing off on their separate lives!'

'You pack a mean punch, Corrie.' Blake moved back to the bench. In the silence the coffee percolator began to burble, steam rising and curling from the spout. Corrie saw the hunching and straightening of Blake's shoulders. Planting his feet squarely, he faced her.

'Corrie, I like you, I admire your spirit, I find you attractive—but falling in love is a luxury I can't allow myself. I can't even promise a long relationship, I have too many other responsibilities.'

She felt despair wash through her.

'Then you know my answer. I'm sorry, Blake.'

Knowing he was not prepared to give a charmer's lie, Corrie looked out of the window at the ever-constant sea. It seemed ironic that in the instant she realised Blake was a man she could love forever, she had denied him. The knowledge seemed a part of her, like the relationship of sea and the shore. Without love he would overwhelm her values, she could become a piece of flotsam, bleached, drained and pitted.

'I'll go home,' she said quietly.

He looked at her, searching her face.

'Not yet—you're pale. You'd better sit down and have some coffee.' He reached down two mugs and began pouring the dark, aromatic fluid.

'Thank you,' Corrie heard her voice sound stiff and formal. 'I don't have sugar or milk.'

'Here you are.' He passed it to her, taking care not to touch her. The loss of his warmth hurt. She made an effort to speak.

'Carting a supply of milk around in a backpack isn't to be recommended,' she said. 'I learnt to go without.'

'Fresh milk and racing yachts don't go far either,' Blake admitted as he walked back to the stove, checked it, then carried the blackened pan to the sink. Water gushed on to it, covering its protesting sizzle. He wiped down the bench and stove, then tried his coffee again.

'How did you get into photography?' he asked.

It was small talk, Corrie realised, heartsore. He didn't really want to know. But she was too shattered to challenge him. It was easier to answer. 'There was a club at school,' she told him. 'A teacher encouraged me to send some of my early photos of Roddy to a local magazine. The art editor wanted more of my work, so I sent some shots I'd taken of the seals in the Bay. He was impressed, called me in and gave me a regular contract. As well, he advised me of other national and international magazines who would be likely to buy my pics. I owe him a lot.'

'You must have been pretty good!' Blake sounded interested. 'Why animals and birds?'

'I'm not sure. I'm always being ribbed about my strays,' she confessed.

'I would never have known it,' Blake smiled, a teasing, understanding in his dark eyes again. Corrie took another mouthful of the hot coffee, gulping it to overcome the quick, sensual response that had leapt through her at Blake's smile. It was important to keep talking.

'Perhaps living here made me aware of them,' she went on. 'I remember my first albatross shots quite clearly. Two birds were gliding over the hill vantage point and I had my camera and four blanks left on my film. When the film was developed it was the albatross ones I was disappointed with, I knew I could do better. I was hooked!' Corrie picked up her coffee. 'Earlier, I'd tried drawing them, but it was too frustrating. Dad was quite deft with charcoal sketches. He used to encourage me and show me tips about perspective and light. Philip was good too: sometimes he's a more objective judge of my work than I am.'

Blake picked up the plate of pancakes from the oven. 'We may as well eat these. Help yourself.' He added the lemon and sugar and the tin of golden syrup. 'Do you take photographs of people?'

'Seldom, although I took quite a few of Misty's twins. James and Matthew were just over three when they came to Hidden Bay. They're irrestistible!' She wasn't aware of her faint sigh. 'I miss them such a lot, Misty too.'

'Another lame duck with her brood? A solo parent, isn't she?'

'Yes. Her husband was spoilt and immature. He abandoned Misty when the twins were a couple of years old. Perhaps he might have improved later, but he got drunk one night and wrote himself off and the girl with him in the car.'

'Misty is an unusual name,' commented Blake.

'It suits Misty well. She's soft and gently and fragile-looking, artistic and poetic. Dark hair and huge eyes, very beautiful. Men fall in love with her on the spot,' Corrie told him.

'But no mathematician! Did you photograph her?'

'Yes, Misty and a camera are naturals together.' Corrie rolled her pancake up and looked at him. 'I'd like to photograph you.'

'Forget it. I've had formal portraits before, and I've loathed them! I prefer the action shots some of the Press have.'

'Despite what you said about freelance photographers?' Corrie couldn't resist the barb. Softening, she spoke slowly. 'A lot of people feel exposed and threatened by a camera. They feel self-conscious. That's why shots taken in their own environment often appeal. They're not in an unnatural setting, and if they're actually involved in doing something familiar then the action reveals more. The art and skill of the photographer comes in selecting the angle, light and composition of the subject in the scene and knowing the possibilities of the camera and the film.' She pulled a grimace. 'Sorry, I don't usually rave on.'

'I'm interested,' said Blake. 'It's always good to talk to someone who's an expert. Particularly over pancakes!'

'I'm not an expert with photographing people. But I would like to try to do a big picture of you—at sea, possibly in a race. You need a challenge, I suspect a windy day would be best!'

'No way!' Blake laughed. 'The last thing I need in a

gale is a photographer getting swept overboard! And knowing you and your affinity with water that's what would happen!'

'I'd promise not to fall overboard!'

'Promises don't come into it. It's not exactly a voluntary movement! The last time it happened I nearly died. The water was freezing!'

'So you knew about hypothermia first-hand.'

'Yes. I've come close to it on board too. That's the reason for the zero suits. Heading towards Cape Horn it pays to be prepared.'

'I can imagine!' Corrie agreed. 'Mine's been so handy since I worked in Antartica.'

'What were you sent there for?' He took a healthy bite of another pancake.

'Photographing penguins. A friend of mine is one of the scientists involved, so he asked me if I'd care to do it. Naturally, I jumped at the chance. Records are kept of the penguin colonies to monitor growth and breeding patterns. The ecology is sensitive to change, so the penguins are a scale indicator. We made flights over the colonies and photographed them. Once that was done it was easy to keep count. Corrie smiled. 'Leaning out of a helicopter to get shots in that temperature gives the word "cold" a new meaning!'

'Icicles on your eyelashes?'

'How did you know?' she laughed.

'I noticed how long they were when you were recovering in bed. I had plenty of time to study you,' Blake told her.

'Wondering if I was going to survive?'

'I was determined you were going to make it.'

'You shouted at me!' she complained.

'I had to reach you. And I was angry!'

'If I'd died here I would have fouled up your privacy

for the boat!' With surprise Corrie realised she had relaxed and was enjoying teasing him. The incidents of the morning, instead of blowing them apart, were like the foundations for a bridge.

'Why do you think I was angry?' The quick smiled flashed.

'Because you were concerned about me.' It was Corrie's turn to smile. 'Life is important to you.' She frowned. 'I seem to recall some incident where you risked your life racing your yacht to pick up some people stranded in the Pacific.'

'It was nothing. The news media made it a big deal. I just happened to be close to the area at the time.' Blake looked at her with eyes that reminded her of a hungry huntaway sheepdog.

'Have the last pancake?' she offered.

'No, thanks. I've had enough.'

Looking through the window, Corrie saw a tall figure down by the boatshed. Blake saw her glance. 'Paul,' he told her. 'He'll be here shortly with the figures.'

'Does he work with you always?'

'No, I wish he would. He's a good sailor and a first-rate administrator. We've known each other since primary school down the road. Sea Cottage was his second home. Dad used to make small boats, so we grew up racing each other in P-class, then we built a cat together.' Seeing her quick puzzlement, he laughed. 'A catamaran! It was a speedy little craft. I gave my share in it to Paul when our family left Hidden Bay. We kept in contact—holidays and so on. He read law at Auckland so he could fit in more sailing—unfortunately a legal career doesn't allow time for a lot of blue water races.'

'Blue water?' queried Corrie.

'Sorry, it just means ocean rather than coastal sailing.' Blake checked his watch. 'He's due any minute with today's print-outs.'

'Where are the crew? I didn't hear the cars start.'

'They're still training on the beach. I do a different exercise programme, thanks to my leg.' He pulled a face. 'If I'm not fit enough in time I'll have to disqualify myself.'

'That will be hard?' she asked.

'Yes.' The simplicity of his answer said a lot. 'It wouldn't be fair on the rest of the team to handicap them. Besides, the "bathtub toy", as you called it, is my special project. The designer and I worked together on ideas and details before the drawing stage. . .the financing alone was a struggle. It gave me the incentive to win my last three races. The Japanese Hawaiian race would have topped it off.'

'So if the yacht isn't a success you could lose a lot of money?'

'The yacht is a success. Already we're setting speed records for the size of the boat.'

'Why is it so important to keep it out of sight?' Corrie asked.

'Competition! Design details are guarded like military secrets. Another designer could copy our ideas and technical advances, possibly improve them further and beat us on the water. Sponsorship is much easier if there's a good chance of being first. *Taiaroa's Petrel* is worth big money. Besides, I like to win!' His admission was charismatic.

'*Taiaroa's Petrel*?' Corrie queried. 'Your name, the headland's and the albatross's, masters of wind and sea. Very appropriate!'

'I'm glad you approve. I wanted to call it something to do with the great birds, but I couldn't come up with the right combination. The possessive appeals.' Blake's eyes reminded her of his nickname for her. . .stormy petrel. Was he saying he wanted to possess her? Or was he telling her that he already owned what he desired, the magnificent racing yacht berthed in Hidden Bay?

CHAPTER SIX

WITH dismay Corrie realised Blake had assumed she had not taken any film of the yacht at any time. She would have to tell him the truth. An icy prickle touched her when she remembered the prints she had entered in the photographers' national competition. If they were placed in their sections they would be displayed in the travelling exhibition.

'More coffee?' he asked.

'No, thanks. Blake. I've something to. . .'

'Corrie—look!' Her confession was cut short by the peremptory command. She looked where Blake pointed, but from her angle she could see only sea and sky.

'Come here! Quick!'

Puzzled by his insistence she went and stood next to him at the window. From there she saw that an albatross had just taken off from the cliff. She glanced at Blake, surprised by his joyful attitude. Living at Sea Cottage, take-offs and landings by the albatross on the cliffs would be a frequent daily occurrence. The albatross was flying over Hidden Bay, his giant wings carrying him on the stiff breeze. Corrie narrowed her eyes, frowning. Never had she seen an albatross fly so awkwardly. Even from her spot she could see that the silhouette of the bird's body was out of line, a leg slow to move into position.

'He's got it now!' Blake exclaimed jubilantly. 'Good on you, mate!'

Corrie watched the bird. A mature albatross with a

ten-foot wingspan, his leg had clearly been injured, yet the bird had within a short time adjusted his wings to compensate and was gaining speed. Experimenting, he circled, and as he came closer to Sea Cottage Corrie gasped. His marking was the same as Roddy's! The sudden reminder brought moisture to her eyes.

'Tears?' Blake's voice was gentle. He slipped an arm round her.

'I'm not crying!' She swept the back of her hand across her face. 'I was just caught unprepared—he looks so much like Roddy. Same markings, but he's smaller in the body. And he doesn't fly nearly as well!'

'That *is* Roddy.'

Corrie could only look at Blake.

'He's not flying as well because he has a pin in his leg. And he's lost body weight because he's hungry. It's almost three weeks since Jenny put him back on his territory. He's learnt to walk again and now he's flying. In a few moments he'll be out to sea having a good meal!'

Corrie felt him study her amazement.

'You didn't know Roddy was alive?'

'Roddy alive!' She found herself hugging him. 'Oh, Blake!'

'You thought he was dead?' Blake was puzzled. 'But surely Jenny or Philip told you? I know he was a doubtful survivor until he flew, but now he'll be fine! Trust me, I'm an expert on legs!'

Happiness lit into shining prisms of joy. It was an instinctive action to lean forward and hug Blake, touching his lips with her own. The passion that had been kept under control exploded with the intensity and blaze of a forest fire after a hot, drought-parched summer.

'Corrie!' Blake breathed her name with a sigh.

Corrie felt his grip tighten around her, his midnight eyes meeting hers until she closed her lids, unable to look at him. His lips covered her mouth, his tongue seeking entry as of right. Her own response was urgent. Curving her body into his, she could feel beneath the texture of his jersey the thick, hard bulk of his body, smell the subtle spice of his aftershave mixed with the warm, healthy male scent. Giving herself up to the sheer pleasure, she groaned as he began trailing kisses down the side of her neck, nuzzling the skin erotically under her ear. Almost roughly he pushed her away.

'Two flies!'

The words and action shocked her as he had intended. It seemed incredible that he had not been as affected as she had been. But the evidence was in front of her, in his stance and angry eyes.

'Who do you think you're playing with, Corrie? You get some sort of kick from your game of advance and retreat?'

Wide-eyed, she looked at him, feeling as if he had winded her.

'Dammit, you know what you're doing!' Blake continued, pounding his fist into his own hand. She bit off her own protest—she had been the one to begin the kiss. 'Look at you!' he roared. 'You stand there looking so fragile and innocent, and you've more sex appeal than a line-up of beauty queens!'

A growing conviction glowed in Corrie. He was angry because he wanted her so much. His own integrity had stopped him—he had respected her beliefs! Of course he should be mature enough to recognise the cause and reason for his anger, but wasn't it a typical male's attitude that he had blamed her? Almost idly she wondered how long it would take him to realise it himself. Recalling his comparison of her with a line-up of beauty queens, she felt like dancing, especially as she was wearing an outfit which could never be described as seductive! Maybe he did love her? He was seeing her as a person he cared enough about to protect. The thought was dizzying. Even as she watched him, she saw his anger quenched, to be replaced by frowning consideration.

'Blake!'

The knock and call coincided. Corrie saw Blake thrust his hand through his hair in frustration, but he spoke naturally enough. 'Come on in, Paul.' He gestured to Corrie. 'Our intruder, my neighbour, Corrie Seton.'

'Good to see you again, Corrie.' Paul grinned. 'More colour than the last time we met!'

'Borrowed plumage,' she smiled. 'I hope one day to meet you when I'm wearing my own clothes.'

'It's getting to be a habit,' laughed Paul. 'So you're here on trial? What's the verdict? Has Blake been using his charm to persuade you not to publish?'

'Corrie's the photographer who took my Taiaroa picture. She's not going to worry us, we're not an endangered species.' Blake smiled. 'Corrie's a nature photographer. She was there because two yellow-eyed penguins have nested in the Bay.'

'Corrie Seton—C. S. You're C. S. The photographer?' Paul was incredulous. 'I imagined you as a backpacking mountain man with a wire wool beard! I'm pleased to meet you officially, I've admired your work for years in the local newspaper. Last week's Pic of the Week comical shot of three seals was a classic!'

'I was pleased with it,' Corrie admitted. 'Seals are great to photograph—natural posers!'

'You've just returned from Australia, haven't you? Photographing the wildlife.'

'Australia, Antarctica!' Blake sounded surprised. 'Where else?'

'My publishers have offices in New York, Toronto, Paris, Munich, Milan, Madrid, Tokyo, London and Sydney.' Corrie ticked off the place names. 'But I usually work in the southern hemisphere. The Galapagos Islands I dream about visiting.'

'Been there! Done that!' Blake and Paul spoke together.

'There are plenty of seals there,' put in Paul.

'And the frigate birds. . .like fighter jets. They do everything except fly backwards.' Blake added, 'Bandits of the sky, Corrie!'

'Unfortunately, it's not the easiest place to visit,' Corrie said, envy in her voice. 'One day I'd like to charter a boat to sail in a line from the Campbell Islands to the Galapagos. I'd end up with a photographic study from the sub-Antarctic to the Equator.'

'Roughly, latitude fifty-two longitude one-six-nine to latitude zero and ninety degrees long.' Blake supplied the figures. 'You'd cover Bounty Island, the Chathams, Bass and Pitcairn, then a long run up to the Equator. It's a trip I wouldn't mind doing myself.'

'I'll keep you in mind,' Corrie smiled. 'But don't hold your breath, I'll probably be a hundred before I can afford it. Which reminds me, I'd better get back to work.' She picked up her camera equipment and rolled up the suit. 'It's all right if I carry on photographing in Hidden Bay?'

'Of course. So long as you don't take pictures of the yacht and the crew, I couldn't care less how long you spend there. Leave the hide, I'll see it's put back into place.'

She hesitated, but Blake moved to take the printouts Paul was holding out, and the moment to tell him about her photos of the yacht and the competition entry was gone.

Paul let her out of the door. She walked back along the road, her backpack heavy, as though the weight of her thoughts had been added like so much lead. The first thing she had to do was to check the date of the contest's closure. If only it was not too late to withdraw her entries. . . Otherwise. . .but it didn't bear thinking about Blake's reaction!

As soon as she had put her cameras and gear away she went to her filing cabinet for the duplicate contest papers. Her eyes scanned the conditions, checking the dates, but, as she had dreaded, the contest had closed. In less than a month the winners would be announced and the prizewinning photos displayed in the major centres in a travelling exhibition.

Would that give Blake enough time? And why was she panicking? Only the prizewinners of each section would be on show. How likely was it that her photographs of the yacht would be winners? She pulled out another file and selected the copies of photographs she had entered.

Her animal study was good, she knew it, and she guessed it stood a better than average chance of being in the top three. She had won the Nature Study section twice before and wanted to win the hat trick. Automatically handling the prints with care, she selected the second photo. The picture of the yacht in the dawn mist would not worry Blake, she decided. Little detail of the yacht could be picked out, merging as it did with the mist. It could be any racing yacht, anywhere; even the distinctive headland of Taiaroa was blunted and shadowed by the sea mist. Relieved, she slipped it back into its protective sheet and then her deft, slim fingers pulled out the action shot.

Dismay deepened as she studied it. Philip had been right: emotion, movement, light and perspective, the classic elements to form a great picture, were contained in the photograph. The focus lay in the balance of the men visible on board, with Blake, partially obscured, forming a point of the triangle. Further emphasising it was the angle of the mast, the taut, swollen belly of the mainsail and the long, sweeping curve of the hull. Triumph and movement glowed in the attitudes of the crew; she had captured the moment of their elation.

It was a good action shot. Corrie grimaced as she placed it under the magnifying lens. The men were side-on or back to the camera or hidden by the sails, but details of the mast with its ribbon markings focused up sharply. She set the lens again and more detail appeared, the apparent solidity of the mast dissolved to reveal strips latticed to a slim core. She frowned, remembering she had noticed the mast and its unusual height. The construction revealed in the photo enlargement could be exactly the type of detail Blake had worked so hard to keep secret. Her fingers edged the photo forward and she studied the details of the rigging. It looked familiar, so she examined the sail. Apart from the odd pattern of the shape it meant nothing to her, but it could mean a lot to others. She pushed the photo around, wryly noting the clarity of the enlarged detail. The film had given good results in the early morning light, combining in perfect synchronisation with distance and shutter speed. If one had been fractionally different the enlargement would not have remained so sharp. Her studies of animals and birds often needed such detail, and she had focused on the moving boat using the same techniques.

She put the photograph back into place and closed the cabinet drawer, as though by doing so she could shut out its existence. What were her chances? Would it be placed in the top three? It was a possibility. The judge would be looking for action, and the photograph had captured it.

She had to tell Blake! But what would she say? And how to explain? Could she leave it until the contest was announced and tell him only if the photograph was successful? The Action category was always a popular one with sports photographers in particular. . .the winning goal, the diving try, the leaping catch. There was also the work of photo-journalists which would cover any moving object. Technically, her photo was first-class, but the standard of other professional entries would also be superior. Although tempted, she knew she would have to face Blake and show him the pictures. Once he studied the photos he would know whether or not they represented any danger to his plans.

First, she needed a shower and a change to her own clothes. An hour later she collected the photos of the yacht and her courage and made her way back to Blake's house. Looking round, she saw an unfamiliar car under the long carport and stopped, uncertain, not wanting to interrupt Blake if he had visitors. It was too late to walk away, the alarm would have told him someone had climbed the gate. She took a deep breath and marched forward to knock on the door.

It was an anticlimax to her rehearsals to have no one answer. She wondered if she should leave the photos with a note, in his letterbox. He would be angry, but after a time he would realise that she had taken the shots from her own property, before she had any knowledge that the project was secret. With a sigh she knew she would have to face Blake, if their relationship was to have a chance. The conviction of its importance was innate. She had never believed in love at first or even second sight, but until she met Blake she had never experienced such powerful, sensual attraction.

At the back of her mind had been the comforting idea of a traditional marriage and home for herself, but when and with whom had never been clear. Blake had kissed her and she had known. The subject had leapt sharply into focus, but Blake had ripped the picture in two. Corrie shook her head. He wanted her, but he had not wanted a long-term commitment, and the joke was that until that kiss she would have protested just as vigorously that she wasn't interested either. She had a career she loved with almost missionary zeal. In her own right she was just as successful, just as hard-working, disciplined and talented.

But if the man she loved was Blake? She found her career thoughts wavering, then smiled with the realisation that she had a career which would match perfectly with Blake's. There would be separations, but much of their work could be planned to fit together. Maybe she would photograph some of the remote parts of the world after all!

She smiled with joy. When they had children. . .they could do so much together. Sea Cottage would always be home. Blake's wife. . . Corrie's husband. . .the words gave a right to love and to be loved.

'Can I help you?'

The stranger's voice shattered her mirror-glass dreams. It took a moment to gather herself to speak. 'I was looking for Blake,' she said.

'Blake's not here.' The man stood resolute, on guard. He must have come from the boatshed. 'He won't be here for a week.'

'Blake's away for a week?' It was a shock, proving

how crazy her fantasy had been. She didn't know Blake at all!

Crushed, she noticed the choppiness of the waves. Although she couldn't see them from Hidden Bay she knew the cause—the wash of two freighters, one leaving and the second going to the port. What was the expression? 'Ships that passed in the night.' Was that to be her relationship with Blake?

Back in the studio she slammed the prints in the file. There was nothing she could do to contact Blake, so the faster she immersed herself in her work, the sooner she would get over the fantasy. It was almost sunset when she felt hungry and glanced at her watch. Surprised by the time, she packed away her photos and walked through to the kitchen, where Philip was preparing dinner.

'Thought I'd make a start. You've been busy!' he smiled. 'Success with the penguins?'

By the time she had told him about the episode with the film Corrie was laughing. She could even chuckle over Blake flipping pancakes, but after that she sobered. The rest was too private. She had to forget. Watching the news on television, she found her thoughts drifting, and when Philip asked her about the weather forecast she had to admit to a blank.

'Go to bed early! It's all the pre-dawn starts,' Philip teased. 'Or was breakfasting with Blake too much for you?'

'I am tired,' Corrie admitted. She thought of one of the pleasant moments of the day. 'Roddy's flying! Why didn't you tell me he was alive?'

'He flew? That's great! We were ninety per cent certain he wouldn't make it. Jenny and I discussed telling you he was alive, but neither of us could bear having to turn around possibly the following day to tell

you he'd died. So when you didn't ask. . . The other
time one had his leg pinned, it didn't work out.'

Corrie sobered, remembering the loss. The telephone rang and Philip moved to answer it. She noticed
the quick eagerness on his face, and his disappointment. She knew he had hoped to hear Misty's voice.

'Jenny? Yes, Corrie just mentioned it. . . He landed
safely? Yes, I'll pass on the message. . . Blake's away?
Checking with the specialists in Auckland. . .'

The half ends of the conversation were obvious to
Corrie, but it hurt when Jenny told Philip the reason
for Blake's absence. Blake had trusted Jenny with the
information. The tiny worm of pique died under her
immediate concern for him. Would he be all right? The
question kept popping to the top of her mind. After
talking to Jenny, Corrie reached for a book she had
been intending to read, but the first chapter involved a
lawsuit for medical damages. Thrusting the book away,
she went out to the kitchen and began preparing two
casseroles. Chopping carrots and onions gave vent to
some of her feelings, and when her 'eyes leaked', as
one of Misty's boys had described tears, she was able
to blame the onions.

In the pre-dawn hours rain pelting down meant she
could stay in bed, and she switched off her alarm clock
with a sigh. Within five minutes she was wide awake
and thinking of Blake. What if the surgeon was worried
about the mobility of his leg? He seemed to be making
a good recovery, but did she really know?

Corrie punched her pillows and pulled the sheet and
duvet up to her chin. She had to put Blake Hanley out
of her mind. He had no intention of allowing her to
disturb him, she reminded herself. So why couldn't she
be equally resolute?

At six o'clock she gave up and decided to shower and dress. The only way she was going to stop worrying about the man was to get back to her work in the studio. Perhaps, after all, her editor would receive her prints on time!

Two mornings later she heard the rain ease and got up to read the cloud-covered sky. If it cleared she might get her penguin shots; much more rain and the penguins' plumage would be spoilt by mud and mess around the nest area, and the brood patches from the egg. Her luck with the hoi-ho seemed to be true to form!

In the dark grey of dawn, light showed in the second bedroom of Sea Cottage, then more lights switched on in the bathroom and kitchen. Corrie watched as the door opened and she recognised her giant. Clearly he had been on security duty. The two cars arrived and soon after the yacht sailed out under Paul's command. She wondered if Blake was lying awake, picturing it.

The sea in Hidden Bay had been lashed into an ugly mood by the rain and winds, and Corrie decided it was just as well Blake could not see the conditions. If sheltered Hidden Bay was rough, the open sea would have hill-high waves. The penguin was late saying goodbye to the female staying on the nest; evidently the cloudy dawn had allowed the bird to sleep longer too. He was in no hurry to enter the water, but the light was not bright enough to film. Thinking regretfully of her warm bed, Corrie had to wait until he entered the sea before shafts of sunlight pierced the clouds.

A familiar bird call made her gasp. Roddy had appeared and was flying only a few feet above her!

'Roddy!' she called.

A small nick in the white feathers above one eye was

sickeningly familiar, but he inspected her with interest as she took several photographs of him.

'Roddy! It's so good to see you flying!' Corrie murmured. 'You wonderful big bird! How's your leg?'

She was able to see the awkward way he held the leg, trying to keep it smooth against his body.

'It will get better, Roddy,' she said softly. 'You and Blake are a good pair!' Another albatross squawked a wary protest and Corrie recognised one of the female birds who had been raised near Roddy's nest. With a soft call Roddy angled his wings to climb up and away before sweeping back beside the female bird. Within seconds the pair were heading for the open sea.

Smiling, Corrie walked back to the farmhouse. Philip was finishing breakfast, and he grinned when he saw her.

'The yellow-eye in the camera? You look happy!'

'No. The light wasn't good enough until a few minutes ago when Roddy flew down to see me. I took a couple of good close-ups. He was with a protective friend. I think they've formed a pair bond,' she told him.

'They won't mate this season.' Philip glanced out of the window which overlooked the sea, but only a couple of gulls were wheeling in the sky. 'I'm glad the weather's clearing. The past three days have been miserable for the late lambs.' He stood up and shrugged on his heavy jacket, then pulled on a balaclava. 'Are you going to town today?' he asked Corrie. 'There's a letter I'd like you to post.'

She nodded. 'I'll go this morning. We need some more groceries and fruit.' She hesitated. Philip seemed his usual smiling, thoughtful self, but there were too many times when the pain showed in his eyes.

'Philip, you had to come home from Christchurch

without seeing Misty. Why don't you forget the farm for a few days and go to see her? I'll check the stock for you. Lambing's virtually over. As long as you tell me which paddocks you want grazed, I can shift the stock around.'

'I'll think about it.' The bleakness was back in his voice and Corrie wished she had said nothing. There was no cheerful whistling as he let himself out and walked over towards the trees where the eagerly barking farm dogs were chained by their kennels.

Corrie delayed her trip to write a quick letter to her mother, then picked up her brother's letter to Misty and put it with her own mail. The drive along the Peninsula coastline usually pleased her, but for once she scarcely noticed the grey-tossed sea as she wondered if there was anything she could do to bring her brother and Misty together. When she had left for Australia she had been expecting them to announce their engagement; on her return it had been a shock to find that Misty and her twins had shifted to Christchurch, over two hundred miles away. Philip had made the trip north intending to see Misty and the boys, but the same day the hospital's call meant he had raced back to Dunedin without seeing them.

Corrie eased her car into the Anderson's Bay traffic and followed it into Princes Street. Her morning passed quickly and she met a couple of her friends for an elastic lunch hour before driving back home. The corners and the twists of the road reminded her of the saying about the path of true love. With Blake their short journey had ended in a sharp, compulsory stop, but Philip and Misty had travelled the same path for almost three years, and Corrie had seen Misty turn from her stress and near despair to a gradual renewal of joy. Philip had been patient and gentle, prepared to give the woman he loved the time Misty had needed.

Corrie stopped at the gate, reached for her key ring, then selected the padlock key. It clicked open and the chain rattled back to free the gate. A swift shove and the drive was clear. It was a pity other stops could not be freed as easily, she mused as she drove the car through. She unloaded the bags of groceries, then garaged the car. Philip was changing the oil filter on his vehicle.

'Thought I'd take up your offer,' he explained, smiling. 'I've written up a sheet of instructions. It's on the kitchen table.'

'I'm so pleased, Philip! When do you leave?'

'Tomorrow. I'll go round the stock early.' He looked at his hands dripping oil and grinned. 'Want me to change your car's oil while I'm about it?'

Corrie shook her head. 'No, thanks, Philip. I haven't done much mileage in the past couple of months. The weeks in Australia and two weeks in bed. . .'

'What some people will do to save petrol!' he mocked. 'By the way, Blake rang.'

'Blake rang?' Corrie stopped in mid-track, her heart thumping crazily. 'Is he all right?'

'He sounded fine.' Philip grinned. 'Disappointed you weren't home!'

Corrie felt a warm glow switch on at the knowledge that Blake had thought of her.

'Apparently he was feeling guilty about the wasted film of the penguins. He suggested that you could build a hide on the other side so you could film at sunset. I told him I'd pass on his message.'

Corrie's warm glow faded as she realised the call had been a business one. 'I did consider it,' she said, 'but coming out of the sea they look like bedraggled, half-drowned little people.'

'It should be fine tomorrow. The barometer is rising.'

Despite her brother's prediction the morning dawned slowly through an overcast sky. Corrie only used her camera to capture six albatrosses flying in a group, like formation pilots in a team display. She was beginning to think that her penguin attempts were doomed to failure. The female penguin stopped to preen before the strip of sunlight and Corrie felt her frustration rise. She held her breath in hope, but the little penguin moved quickly over the sunlit patch. Disappointment surged through her.

The 'hoi-hoi-ho' of the male bird back at the nest caused the penguin to turn. Waddling back, it stopped in the sunlight uttering what sounded like a grumbling enquiry. Corrie worked as the yellow-eye looked up and down, then as the male bird was quiet it began preening, allowing Corrie to frame shot after shot. She was about to change cameras, having finished her first film, when the bird shuffled off to the sea.

Elated, she set off back to the farmhouse. She could hardly wait to begin processing, and ignoring breakfast began to work, her enthusiasm and hope rewarded as the negatives were developed. Nothing had gone wrong! They were sharp and well lit, the composition she had rehearsed for so long had come out exactly as she had hoped, with the penguin a perfect model.

Satisfied, she eased back, her shoulders aching. She switched off her equipment, then went out to the kitchen. The sight of Philip's bag by the outer door pulled her up sharply.

'You just came out in time,' Philip said. 'I gather you caught the yellow-eye?'

'At last!' Corrie picked up two thick slices of kibbled

wheat and popped them in the toaster. 'I'm starving! You ready to go?'

'Yes.'

The single word betrayed his anxiety. Corrie handed over a packet of photographs she had selected. 'Misty might be interested in some of my bird shots. Give her my love, and give James and Matthew a cuddle from me too.'

Philip nodded and cleared his throat. He marched out of the door, head high as though ready to face a hundred dragons. Corrie felt a lump in her throat. Slaying dragons was a task Philip would find straight-forward, but capturing the heart and hand of the 'princess' was a different story. Corrie ate her toast, then tidied the kitchen. The housework had been put on holiday leave, but she no longer had an excuse. She needed a break from her studio as too many hours led to loss of concentration and her penguin prints were important. Emptying the teapot, she rinsed it out, drying it with the rough teatowel until its shiny surface reflected her stretched face smiling back. She put the teapot away on its stand on the bench and glanced out of the window. A dropping in black and white had smeared one small area of glass. The day's next task to clean the window seemed self-selected!

Feeling smugly virtuous, Corrie pulled across the living-room curtains, shutting out the night. The day had been good. The penguin photos had turned out well and the glinting windows of the farmhouse could be forgotten for a few more weeks. And her thoughts of Blake had been kept under control. She wondered if he would ring her again. If only she had been able to talk to him the day before! She stopped, catching herself back from a world of 'ifs and maybes'. There was no point. She wasn't going to sit and wait. Briskly she marched to the telephone and rang Jenny Anderson.

It was after ten when she returned from Jenny's place, and as she shut the garage door she heard the phone ringing in the house. Racing inside, she reached the telephone just as it stopped. For a moment she stared at it, willing it to ring. What if it had been Blake?

The silence mocked her. As she climbed the stairs she persuaded herself that it had been a call from her mother, or Philip, or from any one of several people, or even a wrong number. There was no reason for Blake to ring her, was there?

The dawn saw Corrie at work again. Having captured the female on film she had decided to try for a matching shot of the male. The sunrise was fine with a stiffening chill wind. Corrie found her attention caught by the yacht as it tacked back and forth in Hidden Bay, the crew practising sail changes. She found herself timing their manoeuvres, admiring their slick mastery. Once again the distinctive soft calls of the penguin pair alerted her to her work. The birds were both outside the nest and were walking and talking together, like an old couple in deep discussion. Corrie frowned, worried that they were abandoning the nest. There was nothing she could do, except watch, as they kept shuffling towards the sea. Their departure gave her the opportunity she had considered several times.

After taking the camera off its tripod she slipped it under her jacket, then eased herself off the hide and climbed down on to the barnacle-encrusted rocks. Her movements were cautious; her hands wore scars from her last investigation and the need for quiet was imperative. She checked the birds, but they were still standing, their backs to her, and after edging round another rock she was safe from their view.

Jumping on to the sand, she ran to the ngaio tree. It took her seconds to brush it aside, and using her torch, she bent down to see the egg. The light in the small hollow was too dark for her work, so she set up the shot to use a flash and angled the torch on to full power to provide a softening side light. She took one close-up and one of the nest area before she sidled away, using a leafy branch to break up her footsteps. She didn't relax until she clambered back on the rocks and was able to look down and see the penguins. Both birds were standing in the sunlight strip, their head-bobbing and jerky movements telling Corrie they were anxious.

'Helm a-lee!'

Paul's sharp command made her look seawards. The yacht, instead of heading for the open sea, was cruising across the penguins' corner of Hidden Bay, the shouts of the men carrying on the morning wind. The brightly coloured spinnaker being hoisted intimidated both penguins more, and their calls were sharp and plaintive. Corrie was tempted to shout a warning to the crew, but she knew that would only confuse the frightened birds. She lifted off her harness and took off her camouflage jacket. A wave from Paul told her he had spotted her, so she pushed out her hands in a 'Go away' gesture, then pointed to the penguins. The reaction was swift. The spinnaker was dropped, the yacht gybed and headed away.

The penguins stared after it, and Corrie realised she was missing the chance for pictures of the pair. There wasn't time to reach her hide, so she rested her camera on a rock, zooming in for a medium shot, then taking another of the pair backgrounded by the sea, and as the distant yacht tacked and again flew its spinnaker she took a third. There was no time for a fourth. The female with surprising rapidity hustled back to the nest and alone the male moved towards the sea. Corrie was conscious of the Antarctic-brewed wind as she waited for the nervous bird to enter the waves.

Three hours later she pushed back her chair, satisfied. The shots of the egg and the nest and the penguin pair were up to her standard. Smiling, she picked up the photo of the two birds gazing in apparent disgust at the yacht with its bright spinnaker. Above the male penguin's head she drew a bubble and wrote 'Showoff!' Blake would enjoy it, despite his instruction not to take any pictures of the yacht. She still had to tell him of the competition entries. Her smile faded.

That wouldn't be funny at all!

CHAPTER SEVEN

GOING round the sheep took Corrie two hours, checking the mothering of three lambs took more time, but in the spring sunshine it was a pleasant chore. Returning home, she saw Roddy and his companion flying back to the headland. Even in a few days Roddy had improved. She hoped Blake was making similar progress, then she switched her thoughts deliberately. There was no point in thinking of Blake!

She remembered she hadn't checked the mailbox, and after feeding the dogs she walked up to the gate. As she pulled out the collection of letters and bills she heard a faint mewing sound. Distracted, she stopped to identify the noise. Again the mewing cry came, and crouching down she saw the two black kittens looking up at her, their plaintive calls weak. A scrap of a scarf beside them told her they had been dumped. Corrie felt a gasp of rage that someone could have abandoned them. The kittens were licking her hands, frantic for food, and if she hadn't bothered to check the mail they would have died. Older, they could have survived by preying on the wildlife chicks such as the rare penguin.

Furious with the thoughtless cruelty of some people, Corrie picked the two kittens up and carried them back to the house. It took only a few seconds to warm some milk but a long time to feed them, prepare a box of sand and a sleep carton and to inspect them for disease. Both were females, Corrie noticed, as she rang another friend, the local vet. She booked times for injections and spaying. She would have to give them away; with her lifestyle it wasn't fair to have a house pet, and, spayed and trained, she had found, previous strays stood a chance of a good home.

The bigger one stalked across the room, dived under a chair, then raced back to his litter mate, who promptly ran across to the table leg, his white-tipped tail straight as a mast. 'Come on, Tailor Sailor,' Corrie scooped him up, 'and you too, Footballer,' as she picked up the all-black one, 'You've had enough for one day!'

Surprising her, they settled into the blanket-lined carton after a brief investigation, and when she checked later they were asleep. Corrie glanced at her watch. She had arranged an outing to the movies with friends, but she would have to cancel. She couldn't leave her foundlings on their first night, but felt pleased with her excuse, honest enough to know she wanted to be at home in case Blake rang.

When the phone rang a few minutes later she raced to answer it, hope in her eyes. Her brother's voice was a disappointment.

'Corrie? You'll never guess!' Philip was ecstatic. 'Misty's going to marry me!'

'That's wonderful news, Philip!'

'I still can't believe it!' His voice was tinged with wonder, but Corrie heard Misty chuckle in the background.

'Hello, Corrie!'

'Misty? I'm so happy for you and Philip.'

Philip came back on the line. 'Listen—I'm staying in Christchurch for a couple of days. Can you manage there?'

'Of course! What can I foul up in two days!' Corrie laughed.

'You want me to answer that? How many baby seals are in the bath?'

It was good to hear Philip so light-hearted. 'I promise there won't be a baby seal!' she smiled, hoping her brother would not ask about other strays. Diversionary tactics were in order. 'I don't suppose you've worked out just when and where you'll get married?'

'Fairly soon. We'd both like the ceremony at Beach Farm. Besides, the boys can't wait to get back.'

'Tell them I missed them and I'm looking forward to their return. Philip, I really am pleased!' Corrie replaced the receiver, after a few more minutes' conversation. With something of a shock she realised she had to find somewhere to live. And another studio. But where?

There were many holiday homes further along the peninsula, but usually the owners wanted to move in themselves over the summer months. Her expensive equipment was not designed to be easily dismantled, so the prospect of packing and repacking held no appeal. She picked up the paper and began reading the 'To let' advertisements. All were located in the city, and Corrie pulled a lugubrious face. She did not want to live away from the sea. The 'For Sale' advertisements looked more interesting, with three properties located down the peninsula. The after-hours number was answered promptly, and it took only a few minutes to fix a time.

The following afternoon, full of anticipation, Corrie drove to the appointed meeting. The house for sale was hidden behind a neighbour's thick macrocarpa hedge, and the same hedge blocked most of the view. The second house had rotting boards, and the home-handyman repairs convinced Corrie she could do better if she looked further. The agent told her the third house on offer had been sold. Disappointed, she drove back to Beach Farm, pessimistic about finding a place to suit.

At home the kittens welcomed her accusingly as if she had left them for days instead of a couple of hours. Their anxious cries ceased only after their small, furry bodies had been cuddled and fed, and the task reminded her to check the lamb and the reluctant mothering ewe she had roped to the fence earlier. After changing into jeans and shirt and pulling on a jacket she walked outside, and the lambing 'eye' dog padded into position beside her. The sight of the lamb sucking, its tail wagging in double joy time, lifted her mood. She walked down to the beach fence, observing the other grazing ewes and their lambs. Further out to sea several albatrosses were wheeling and soaring in a sky party, but the birds were too far away to identify, and the dog, tongue hanging out, brown eyes surveying the sheep, reminded her she had more work to do before locking up for the night. The long twilight had darkened by the time she had finished and was ready to begin her own meal.

It was a soft, water-colour morning of pale blue, thought Corrie as she gazed through the kitchen window to the sea. The mewing of the kittens called her away from the rainwashed scene, and she prepared their breakfast of milk and fish, absently noting how quickly the two had grown. Once fed, they played around her ankles as she wrote the list of chores she hoped to complete before Philip's return. The first was to inspect the paper's 'Houses for Sale' column. Having read it, she frowned. She was beginning to understand why the yellow-eye was such a rare bird. There were not many vacant waterfront homes close to the bush, sheltered from the prevailing wind and totally private!

In the middle of her spring-cleaning Corrie heard a knock at the door. Surprised, as she hadn't heard a car arrive, she took a moment to remember the padlocked road gate. 'Coming!' she called as she ran downstairs, almost tripping over the black kitten lying in wait on the bottom stair. Grabbing him up, she opened the door.

'Blake!' she exclaimed.

Her feelings leapt into a dizzying dance. She wanted to throw herself into his arms, she was so pleased to see him. Instead convention held her and she stood still.

'How are you, Corrie?' Blake looked at her, but his hand went to the squirming kitten. It settled as he tickled it under its ear, its purring an orchestrated symphony of happiness.

'Do you mind if I sit down?' He gestured to the kitchen chair. 'The walk was longer than I thought.'

'Of course! I'll make a drink.' Corrie filled and plugged in the kettle, trying to keep her emotions from bubbling too. Once Blake had sat down the kitten settled on his lap. As its sister jumped up for its share of attention Blake laughed.

'What is this? Invasion by strays?'

'Only two. You don't know a good home for them? They're quite appealing,' Corrie assured him.

'I can see that.' Blake continued to fondle them before putting them back into their box. 'I'll ask the crew tomorrow. It's so good to be home. I hadn't realised until I left Sea Cottage how much I'd missed it.'

'Jenny told us you'd gone to see the specialists.' She tried to sound noncommittal.

'Just a check-up—routine,' he told her.

'The specialist is pleased with your progress?'

'Yes. No one's happier than me. Walking's a bit of a pain, but I can feel the improvement.' His deep brown eyes studied her. 'You look as if you were busy!'

'I am! But I'm glad to stop. I'm being a houseproud Hannah! You must hear the news,' she added. 'Philip and Misty are getting married.' She saw his surprise.

'Misty Harrender? The woman who used to rent Sea Cottage?'

Corrie nodded. 'Philip's coming back tonight, so I've been spring-cleaning.'

'Will you stay here?' he asked.

'No, it wouldn't be fair once they're married. I've been to see a couple of houses for sale, but I'll have to keep looking. I don't want to shift twice, but I'll have to rent rooms somewhere until I can buy or build.'

'There'll be flats in Dunedin,' Blake pointed out.

'I know. But I want to stay near Taiaroa if I can.'

'Not enough lame ducks in town?' he smiled.

'Try albatrosses and penguins!'

'When's the wedding?' he asked.

'I don't know yet.'

'It could be months away!'

'Not my brother—he's an action man! And he's wanted to marry Misty for a long time.'

'Forgive my lack of enthusiasm,' Blake said sardonically. 'Marriage holds no interest for me! That sort of commitment is not in my plans for the next five years.'

'You've got it all worked out?' Corrie set down cups and saucers, glad that the task gave her the opportunity to move around.

'In five years I shall be past my best at yacht racing, so then I'll look around for some little obliging, dutiful, good-looking woman to marry. . .' he teased.

'You are not funny!' she cried crossly.

'No? But I'm honest. I only play on my terms. I've no intention of sailing into emotional storms.'

Corrie could feel his gaze on her like a caress. What was he saying? His eyes spoke a silent language of love, but his words were a warning. She looked away and tried to be flippant. 'I'm surprised you risked visiting me,' she said. 'What did you call me? A Mother Carey's chicken? A storm warning?'

'You're right. But the distance to exercise my leg was only a little further than the physio recommended.' Blake broke off and smiled, his dark eyes alight. 'All right, I'll admit it! I wanted to see you.'

'A temporary aberration?'

'Yes. Not one I'm finding easy to deal with at present. I continually find my thoughts reverting to you.'

Corrie put down the teapot and glanced out of the window before turning back to him. 'It's either laugh or cry! I'm attracted to you, more than I've ever felt drawn to anyone. A minute ago I was jealous of the kittens. You held and caressed them. But then you put them away in the box, so they couldn't escape to force your attention.'

'You can't be played with and picked up just when I feel in the mood?'

'I'm worth more,' she said firmly.

He stood up, careful not to touch her. 'You could be right, Corrie. I think I'd better go.'

Corrie felt like tears, but she forced them back as he walked to the driveway, his limp more pronounced, his left leg dragging. 'Wait—I'll drive you back,' she said. She wanted to be furious with him instead of being able to understand him. The keys were hanging ready by the door, and she flicked them up into her palm and ran to open the garage. Blake kept on walking and had reached the padlocked road gate by the time she drove up. He stood leaning against the strainer for support, and she had a flashback of him leaning against the bedroom door, physically exhausted after the rescue. Then he had been grey under his tan, his dark eyes open to her gaze. His eyes were hooded, only the taut skin around his mouth betraying him. Corrie opened the padlock, slipped the chain and it rattled against the wire, striking every link. Her emotions were being battered and struck too. She didn't know how Blake could imprint his desire without even touching her, he was so close. The faint scent of his aftershave and the male muskiness of his body tantalised her. She made an attempt to contain the situation. She could not look at him, knowing her breathing was ragged and guessing he could read her emotions. She pushed at the gate, using it as a barrier to move away from him; left foot forward, right foot forward, knuckles white on the paint-flaking metal top bar of the gate, eyes focused on the spikes of grass, bright green, fluorescent lime-emerald in the hot sun.

Jerkily, a wooden puppet, she crossed back to the car, and swung up into the driver's seat. Gripping the steering wheel, she drove the car through the gateway, then heard the clang and shiver of the gate as Blake shut it. She drew several deep breaths, the gate had seemed symbolic. Had she left her home behind, to travel forward with Blake? How far was she prepared to go?

Blake swung into the passenger seat. She knew he was watching her. A stray curl flicked at her cheek and she brushed it away, memory lightning-fast replaying the tenderness when Blake had moved a similar curl for her. Clashing first into second gear made her concentrate on her driving. She wished she could make some witty remark to break the tense consciousness between them, but it was impossible. Blake's gate was a barrier across his driveway.

'I'll drop you here, Blake.' Relief cracked in her voice.

He pulled a remote control device from his pocket. The gate clicked open, swinging back in obedience to the signal.

'You control how close someone gets to you,' Corrie commented.

'Yes. You'll find it easier to turn inside.'

She drove along the bush-overhung drive, stopped the car outside the doors of Sea Cottage, but kept the motor running. 'Are you coming in with me?' Blake's voice was gentle, and her resolution quavered. 'You want me as much as I want you.' He made it a statement. She could not deny it. She was a tightrope-walker balancing on the high wire.

'I'm not sure I can explain,' she said. 'For me it would be a total commitment. Yet I feel as if I'd be making a mistake. I don't know you, Blake. Most people go through a period of getting to know each other and their families, their mutual interests, finding out the things they like and dislike, learning to communicate and trust, developing the relationship. But it's not been like that with you and me. Instead there's been the unbearable ache for each other. I'm running scared. I know you enough to realise that for you, sex with me would be just a brief, pleasurable satisfaction.' She gazed at him, meeting his dark eyes. 'You don't want to care about me—that's one of the few things I do know.'

Blake's hand reached for hers. 'I said more than I realised when I called you a petrel, Corrie. The alba-tross of Taiaroa mates for life. You want me to swear love for you.' He sat, quiet, his eyes watching the waves rise, curl and break. When he turned to face her she knew his decision. 'Corrie, I can't allow myself to love you. The price is too high.'

Hands on the doorframe, he jumped out, the movement eased by his powerful shoulders. Limping, he walked to the cottage door and seconds later it had shut behind him.

Corrie sat, paralysed by his perception and his rejection. If Blake had kissed her. . .

But he had demanded a decision based on will, not sexual attraction. Shouldn't she respect him for that? Or should she be furious? Wasn't it just self-protection? A guarantee that after they had made love. . . 'Made love'. . .the term grated. Blake had ruled out love, only sex. . . After they had had sex she would not ask or expect further involvement. His commitment was to his yacht and his crew. She felt as if the inside of her body was being crushed. She had to get away!

The starter motor's whirring shocked her into realising the engine was still running. She swung the vehicle round to drive out of the gate. Its metallic clang behind the vehicle rang like hollow laughter as she headed back home. Abandoning the car outside the farmhouse, she decided to climb to the lookout. She needed the blast of fresh air to clear her mind and the largeness of the hills to put everything into perspective. Her footsteps slowed as she climbed higher up the cliff, but the physical effort was freeing the tearing pain.

Once she reached the top, the wind slapped, pushed and buffeted her, forcing her to seek shelter from the nearest rocks. Crouching down, she regained her breath, surprised by her own lack of foresight. A stiff breeze at the farmhouse meant a roaring Antarctic gale on the headland.

Her breathing steadier, she looked around. The view
showed the blue Pacific bounded by the sky, the
seabirds flying in the great dome. In the other direction
she could see the miles of the peninsula with the
dramatic hills of the Otago harbour, houses set like
colourful flowers in a border along the lower edge.
Gradually the immensity of the land and seascape
began to help. Was it only a few weeks earlier that she
had stood in the same spot watching Roddy's return?
And her first collision with the owner of Sea Cottage?
She glanced down to Hidden Bay, seeing the high water
almost peaking. Like the sea, Blake had occupied more
and more of her thoughts. She wanted to be angry with
him, but instead she was furious with herself for being
able to understand.

Was it possible to love someone she hardly knew?
She pondered the question and decided that it held as
many answers as the sea held waves. The slap of the
water on the boatshed reminded her of the photos of
the yacht. She still had to tell Blake about them. The
thought of facing his dark, searching eyes and seeing
his expression seared. His opinion of photographers
was not going to be improved.

If only she hadn't sent in the competition entries! If
only the competition hadn't closed, if only she. . .
What if she rang the secretary of the Association and
asked her to withdraw the Action and Romance entries
for personal reasons? The idea was so simple and so
obvious she doubted if it could be so straightforward.
She knew the secretary from other occasions, so there
would be no harm in telephoning her to ask if it was
possible, would there? The secretary was a hard-working woman who was the quiet source of organisation
and detail; she would almost enjoy the lecture she
would give Corrie, but, after it, she would lift her

relentlessly reliable shoulders and the two offending entries would be removed.

Excited, Corrie stood up, then noticed a car towing a trailer-sailer manoeuvred round the sharp turn into their side road. The occasional local boatie had used the drive access to the beach at Hidden Bay, but she didn't recognise either car or boat. They would soon have to stop, their plans thwarted by the electronic gate, and if they tried to turn such a long rig in the narrow road they would end up with one or other vehicles ditched. Their only choice was to go into Beach Farm and utilise the road paddock. . .but access there was padlocked too. The phone call would have to wait a few minutes while she unlocked the gate. Unless the trailer-sailer was being delivered to Blake?

She leaned over to check and saw him walking across the courtyard, and she waited to see if he allowed the rig entry. The gateway was screened by the trees, but after a few moments the car and boat edged along the driveway and stopped in the courtyard. A young woman in dazzling red danced from the car, pirouetted around Blake, then spun away to exult in the view. Blake went and stood beside her, his arm reaching around her shoulder.

A burning fear shot through Corrie and she recognised jealousy. It was not an emotion she had previously known. And what was she doing, spying on Blake? Tormented, she made her way back down the cliff, knowing there could be a thousand reasons for the girl's arrival. By the time Corrie reached the farmhouse she had ripped a fingernail, marked her jeans with a grass stain and her lungs were rasping with each breath. The warmth of the farmhouse restored her, and she persuaded herself that Blake could have a dozen friends who would utilise his jetty for their boats.

In the studio she pulled out the copy of the contest form to check the numbers before telephoning.

'It's Corrie Seton speaking.'

'Hello, Miss Seton. I see you've entered in other sections of the contest this year.' The quick lightness of the secretary's tones was distinctive and familiar, and Corrie crossed her fingers.

'Actually I'm calling you about the other two entries,' she said.

'Miss Seton, you know I can't discuss the contest.'

'Of course. I want you to withdraw my entries in the Romance and Action categories,' she explained. 'I realise I'm asking a lot, but I do have a serious personal reason.'

'Miss Seton. . .' the tide of words gushed over Corrie, but finally the secretary slowed '. . .the preliminary judging has just been completed. Tomorrow the unsuccessful entries will be returned and the rest will be couriered on to the chief judge. I'll ask the committee to withdraw your entries in the Romance and Action categories. It should be straightforward, but I hope you're not going to ask me to post them back urgently. I haven't scheduled any posting until after the contest.'

'That's quite all right,' Corrie said hastily. 'I'm so grateful—thank you very much!'

'I trust you know what you're doing!' The telephone clicked and Corrie replaced the receiver with a gusty sigh of reief. Almost light-headed, she ran upstairs to change into another outfit to make her planned trip to the shops.

On her return she could not stop herself from glancing into Blake's yard as she drove past. Car and trailer-sailer sat parked under the long carport, but the rest of the area was screened by the trees. She tried to tell herself that it didn't mean the girl was still at Sea Cottage, but her tormented imagination supplied her with vivid impressions.

What was happening to her? She had a sudden flashback of watching penguins a year earlier. A female penguin has sashayed up to a male in his nest area and he had appeared to strut and display until his mate arrived home. Her dismissal of the newcomer had been swift and aggressive. At the time Corrie had found the incident comic, but, since seeing the girl in red, she understood the bird's action in driving off the intruder. Like the newcomer penguin, she had to depart without defending herself. She had no claim on Blake and he had none on her.

It was fortunate that Philip arrived home soon after and she had to concentrate on his shining happiness. Even his discovery of the kittens was a cause of laughter, and it was Philip who suggested they would make good pets for Matthew and James, a thought that Corrie, knowing how Misty had wished the boys could have had pets at Sea Cottage, immediately endorsed!

Dressed in warm clothes in the pre-dawn, Corrie set up her cameras. As the light filled the eastern sky she tried not to look at Sea Cottage, although the carport could not be seen from her position. The arrival of the crew emphasised the normality of the routine, so it was a shock to see the trailer-sailer being reversed into the water. One of the crew led the boat out to the jetty and tied it in place, and a minute later Paul Greywood met the young woman and Blake at the door of Sea Cottage. The girl had obviously spent the night.

Dry-eyed, stomach taut with misery, Corrie watched as the girl laughed and talked with several of the crew. It was proof that the relationship with Blake was

familiar and accepted. The pair climbed aboard the
sailer and Blake checked the gear while the girl began
clipping the sails into place, the bright yellow life-jacket
and yachting overalls obvious against the grey of the
sky and the water. Paul and the rest of the crew guided
the silver yacht towards the open sea, but Blake and
the girl put on a display in the trailer-sailer of expert
skill as they changed tack and raised and lowered the
spinnaker, their movements precise and practised, until
they followed *Taiaroa's Petrel*.

Corrie felt a knife-twisting anger savage her. How
could Blake have proposed making love to her when
he was so involved in a long-term relationship? And
she had thought him honest!

The indignant squawk of the male penguin was a
reminder that she was there to photograph penguins,
not to watch Blake. Almost without thought she took
the picture and sat unmoving until the penguin plopped
happily into the sea.

Blake could have a dozen girlfriends! Hadn't she
already rejected a physical relationship? The girl's
arrival had proved her instinct correct, so why was she
feeling so angry? Why did it hurt so much?

Gathering her equipment, she began trekking over
the rocks. Her foot slipped on a piece of seaweed and
she jumped clear, her ankle wrenching badly. The pain
made her concentrate and, taking more care, she
headed back to Beach Farm. Once there she could not
stop herself from looking out to sea.

The two yachts were there, the smaller forcing the
larger to tack or gybe. Corrie was puzzled until she
realised *Taiaroa's Petrel* was sailing on just a storm jib
and double-reefed mainsail, handicapping itself. The
manoeuvres showed Blake's mastery of both boats'
good and bad points. Several times the silver yacht

took valuable seconds to reposition itself, but Paul was quick to counter and always sliced ahead, the *Petrel* faster even with its reduced sail area and a short course.

Corrie turned back to the farmhouse. She had seen enough. She had to tell Blake about the photos, but there was no longer any concern that they could be published, so there was no particular hurry. She had no intention of visiting while he was entertaining his guest!

For the rest of the day Corrie worked on the Australian series, setting the large prints out in rows on the floor of the lounge and the adjoining living-room, much to the scampering delight of the kittens. The area enabled her to compare and arrange possible combinations, but after one of the kittens disgraced herself they were banished.

'I cooked dinner, do you want yours on a tray?' Philip interrupted her and glanced at the photos. 'You've got enough for a mammoth book there—one of those glossy coffee-table types. . . What about it?'

'It's a possibility,' Corrie conceded, 'but the text could be a problem.'

'You've got your diary—and the letters you wrote to Misty and me were fascinating. You write texts for your other photo-essays and editors have been pleased with them. I don't see any difficulty.'

Corrie stood up smiling when she looked back at the carpet of photos. 'I do!' She began collecting them in order. 'Maybe you're right.' Following her brother, she walked to the kitchen. The kittens promptly wound themselves around her feet. Philip had set her meal by the window end of the long work table.

'Thanks, Philip, it smells great!' she told him.

'Your turn tomorrow!' he grinned. 'I met Blake when I was checking the beach paddock this afternoon. He was out walking exercising his leg—quite pleased with himself. He crossed over the rocks!'

'That was stupid of him!' Corrie could visualise only too easily what could have happened. 'Those rocks are treacherous, slippery with seaweed. What if he'd stepped on the scoria?' She stopped, aware of Philip's amused expression.

'And you scamper over them every day!'

'Eat your dinner!' she reminded him. 'It's good!'

'You're changing the subject.' Philip looked sober. 'Just be careful on the rocks, Corrie. If you fell you could be in big trouble. Blake said much the same. Incidentally, I asked him to come for dinner tomorrow night.'

'You didn't!' The thought of polite socialising appalled Corrie.

'Relax, he has a prior engagement.' Philip grinned as he reached for more potatoes. 'Why did it worry you?'

'I'm just a little busy at the moment,' she said severely. 'And the Fiordland trip is coming up soon.' She handed over the bowl of garden-fresh spinach. 'I told him about your engagement.'

'Yes, he wished me well, et cetera—told me he's a great believer in marriage.'

'He said that!' Corrie exclaimed, wide-eyed. 'The hypocrite!'

'Blake a hypocrite?'

'Of the hippopotamus size,' Corrie snorted. 'He's got no intention of getting married for five years.'

'That doesn't mean he doesn't approve of marriage. Simply that he's planned his position. . .and that he's never been in love, of course.' A familiar theme on the television set in the corner broke into their conversation. 'Shh! Here's the news.'

As Philip watched, Corrie fumed, her thoughts burning. She gathered the plates and began stacking them in the dishwasher, running taps and banging and cleaning pots until Philip protested, his gaze never leaving the flickering coloured images. What had he meant about Blake's never having been in love? How could he make such a statement? With a self-righteous slam of the cupboard door Corrie finished tidying and, followed by the two kittens, stalked outside. The evening air with its slight salt taste calmed her, but it was the mewing of the kittens that made her realise she had walked to the beach. As they experimented with the sand, licking it off their coats, she sat on a bench formed by two rocks.

'I was hoping you'd come, Corrie.'

Blake's voice startled her. He sat beside her, his dark gaze checking and caressing her face. 'I was watching for you.' His voice was a murmur like the sound of the sea.

A thousand bitter questions stuck in her throat. She wished there was more room on the seat, but was caught by the edge of the rock and by the closeness and warmth of his body next to hers.

'Look at me, Corrie!'

She turned her head, struggling to maintain an uncaring façade.

'Don't pretend!'

His hands reached out and held her head, and his mouth covered hers. The kiss drew them together, Corrie winding her arms around him, unable to resist the deep, sensual, tactile pleasure of holding him, and being held, her whole body attuned to his, her lips moist and warm on his, deepening and echoing the demands of his mouth, the world of sea and sand spinning into a whirlpool of sensation where all she knew was the touch and warmth and smell of the man she wanted.

'My stormy petrel, my joy, my Corrie!' Blake's voice was a velvet sound on her ear. His lips moved over the delicate skin below her ear, then returned to her mouth with a slight groan, his desire fed by their passion. A sharp prickling and clawing at her feet penetrated Corrie's thoughts, as a kitten tried to climb her jeans.

What was she doing? She had to be crazy, kissing Blake! Roughly she pushed him away

'Stop it, Blake!' She was furious, hurt with pain from the kitten's claws, but more with anger with herself and Blake. 'How could you!'

To her dismay Blake seemed surprised.

'Don't look so innocent!' she snapped. 'I'm not naïve. What about your current live-in love? Doesn't she satisfy you?'

CHAPTER EIGHT

SPLUTTERING with rage, her breasts taut, her body stiff, Corrie hurled questions and accusations like hissing spears. 'Do you think an easy conquest makes you more of a man? It's part of your win-at-any-cost mentality! Feelings and emotions don't matter to you!'

Blake's expression had changed from shock to amusement. His smile devastated her, and she crumpled, turning away in a searing agony. His hands went to her shoulders and held her, imprisoning her.

'Let me go!' her voice faltered, revealing her exhaustion and misery. 'I know your attraction. I can't blame the woman, she probably loves you. But I thought you had more integrity.'

'My sister does love me. The same way you love your brother Philip.'

'Your sister?' Stunned, Corrie looked at him. 'Blake—I'm sorry!' She melted against him. 'I was so angry with you, so hurt. . .'

'I know, it's all right. . .' His kiss was tender. 'I'm sorry I didn't mention that she was coming. It never entered my mind that you'd see her. She'd intended flying back last night, but she couldn't resist the chance of seeing *Taiaroa's Petrel* in action.'

'And she was impressed?'

'Yes—and so was I! *Taiaroa's Petrel* not only looks good, she performs magnificently; fast, yet stable in difficult conditions. I've yearned and dreamed for so long. The Round the World is the race she's been built to win. . .'

Corrie felt cold. Blake did not belong to any woman, but wasn't he besotted by his yacht?

'She does look beautiful,' she agreed.

Blake looked at her. 'Jealous of a bathtub toy, my sweet?'

'I think so. It's so important to you.'

His answer was a swift, passionate kiss that made all her fears thistledown in a wind. 'Better?' he murmured the question, his voice deep, his eyes moonlit shadows.

'Much better,' she sighed, as he drew a line from her ear to her mouth, then dropped a perfect kiss on her lips.

'You'd better go, my stormy petrel, or otherwise take the consequences.'

'I'm going, I'm going,' she said, her voice soft, but stopped to take another kiss.

'I'll walk you back to the farmhouse, make sure you're safe,' he said.

It was a new delight to feel cherished and protected. Blake picked up the kittens and handed them to her, then wrapped them all in one armful. Not for the stars would Corrie have told him that his stride was too large, but an extra step caught his attention and he slowed.

'Guess my leg's better than I realised.' His eyes were full of chuckles. 'You'd better watch out, young woman!' His fingers caressed her shoulder.

'Don't worry, I will,' Corrie smiled as one of the kittens moved an exploratory paw to investigate his hand. Blake withdrew it with a swift motion.

'I've the feeling I'd better watch myself around you!' he grinned.

Moments later the lights of the farmhouse, shining like anxious eyes, lit them to the door.

'I'll see you tomorrow, little petrel.' Blake dropped

a kiss on her hair, swept the curl back from her ear, then turned and strode off into the deepening night.

Elated and uncertain in turn, Corrie walked into the farmhouse. Philip was engrossed in the local news, and she marvelled that the world could have changed so much for her, yet apparently had not affected anyone else. Unless it was Blake? She shivered with joy. She would see him tomorrow! When and how were thoughts that kept her heart singing.

'Corrie, it's Blake. Are you free for a couple of hours?'

'I've got work waiting, but I'd be pleased to take time off, Blake.'

'Good. Meet me at the jetty—bring a thick jersey or a windbreaker and a pair of white-soled sneakers.'

'We're going sailing?' she asked.

'Scared?'

She hesitated before answering him. She wasn't afraid of the sea but of being alone with Blake and her own sky-rocketing emotions. 'I'll see you as soon as I can.'

She replaced the receiver, wrote Philip a brief note, then ran up the stairs two at a time. She packed her waterproof bag, with the jersey, and for good measure wore her windbreaker. Earlier she had put on her favourite pale blue shirt and jeans just in case Blake called at the farmhouse. The aluminium camera case with her range of lenses and films she retrieved from the studio on her way to the garage. Blake hadn't said anything about not taking a camera and she would be able to tell him about the yacht photographs. The gate to Sea Cottage was open, and she drove into the courtyard and parked by the carport.

The sight of Blake in a blue and white striped rugby

jersey with matching blue trousers made her realise how long the morning had been.

'Good afternoon, Corrie.' His smile caressed her as he opened the car door. 'I'm glad you came.'

'With or without the camera?' Corrie smiled a greeting, wondering if Blake could hear the noisy thumping of her heart.

He took her bag, 'It appears to be a case of "Love me, love my camera."'

'You'll let me bring it?' she asked.

'I'm positive I should reply in the negative,' he grinned, 'but it's Be Nice To Corrie Day. I wouldn't have known, but I saw it marked on my desk calendar.'

Rainbows of happiness arced across her private world. She shouldered her camera case, the hard edges bumping against her thighs as they walked across the beach to the jetty.

'Just a minute,' said Blake. 'I'll have to adjust the alarm.'

'You've got the jetty rigged?' asked Corrie.

'It's just a precaution. Once here it would be easy to get on to the yacht. We'll use the trailer-sailer, it's easily handled by one.' He climbed down the metal ladder on to the yacht, dropped the bag, reached out to take her camera case and put it down with exaggerated care before holding out a hand to her. Barely touching him, Corrie watched the slight movement of the water rocking the boat, them jumped.

'Welcome aboard!' smiled Blake as he pressed the starter-motor into action and then hauled up two buoyancy vests. He passed one to her and strapped his own on, then bent to cast off the heavy anchoring ropes.

'Think you can take her out?' he asked. 'I'll get the sails up.'

Corrie looked at the tiller and then back at Blake.

'You can do it, petrel.'

Feeling rather like an albatross about to fly from the cliff for the first time, she adjusted the motor and the boat began to move, nosing back towards the jetty as though reluctant to leave. She edged the tiller over, relieved when the boat responded, and turned towards open water. A few minutes later Blake switched the motor off. 'Head to the point—with this slight wind we'll have to tack to get into the main harbour.'

As she turned the boat, the sails filled and Blake winched the jib sheet and adjusted the mainsail, then settled himself, aparently content to watch her. She was concentrating too hard to do more than risk an anxious smile. The yacht felt so different once the engine had been switched off, and she was vulnerable, conscious that she knew nothing of the power of the wind driving the yacht. Gradually she began to enjoy the experience, discovering the thrill of allowing the yacht more and more wind until she reached a point where the yacht seemed to sing through the waves. When she pushed the tiller a little harder she immediately felt her mistake and edged it back, her hand feeling the slight patterns of the current through the tiller.

'Why did you do that?' Blake looked at her.

'It felt wrong,' she admitted, 'as though there's an unseen groove where we could go fast and the yacht rode well.' She pushed the tiller again and experienced the same sensation as she again corrected it. 'It's like a balance point, I think, Blake.'

'The ability to feel the boat's response is one of the marks of a steersman. You'd be surprised how many lack the sensitivity,' Blake commented. 'Corrie, I'll show you the first tack, then you can carry on.'

Seconds later, their course set to the harbour chan-
nel, Blake handed the tiller back to her. Beyond the
line of the spit and the headland the waves came
towards them in a different pattern, and Corrie found
she was constantly watchful to balance wind and wave
with sail. Blake sat beside her, occasionally adjusting
the angle of the tractor controlling the mainsail or
leaning forward to slacken the jib sheet fractionally.

'You're as natural a sailor as a seagull, Corrie!' he
praised.

'It's fun,' she answered, her eyes sparkling, 'much
better than the runabout! Though Philip's never going
to believe it!' She glanced back towards the headland.
'It looks like a papier-maché model from here. I've
never been as far out as this: usually we stay inside the
harbour.'

'A stormy petrel is at ease on the open sea,' he
reminded her, laughing. 'There's a group of albatrosses
to your right.'

'A water party!'

'Roddy's there too!' Blake added.

'I want to see, but how do I turn the boat off?' Corrie
laughed.

'Think about it.'

Warily she altered the course and the sails began to
lose their curve. Blake's smile told her she was correct
and he adjusted the sails so their progress past the
water party was slow and quiet. He handed her the
binoculars he had been using and she watched the birds
splashing and diving.

'Blake, this is marvellous—the yacht doesn't seem to
disturb the birds. I've never seen a water party up close
before.'

Gradually they left the giant birds behind, and the
swell took on a definite rhythm. Blake showed her how

to handle the sheets which controlled the sails, and she experimented happily, putting the boat into giant circles and changing tack on Blake's instruction.

'You're a good teacher,' she told him.

'Not usually!' he chuckled. 'I think the pupil was a natural. But we'll head back for afternoon tea. Do you think you can put her about?'

Corrie turned sharply, then began cruising back, allowing the craft to run before the wind. 'This is unbelievable, Blake!'

He met her smile with his own, warm and relaxed. 'The weather and wind must have known it was Corrie's Day.'

'It's so quiet,' marvelled Corrie, 'so peaceful.'

Two seagulls screamed overhead, making a mockery of her words, and she joined in Blake's laughter.

'Turn towards the south coast, Corrie,' he instructed. 'There's a small inlet with a jetty we can use.'

'You want to land there? Someone might see you.'

'It's a risk I'll take.'

The gentleness of his expression with his tanned skin crinkling into a smile around his eyes set her heart racing.

'I feel as if we could sail away like the Owl and the Pussycat,' she told him.

'If you're the Pussycat, does that make me an owl?' he mimicked an owlish expression.

She laughed. 'You're a Taiaroa albatross, a master of wind and sea.' Automatically she corrected the slight flap as the breeze gusted. 'How did you become a yachtsman? Was it something you always wanted to be?'

'As a youngster I thought I'd carry on making boats with Dad,' he told her. At some stage I realised he was spending more and more time in the factory and less

and less on the water. When I reached university I
started study in marine biology. I dropped out of the
course two-thirds of the way through—an exam clashed
with an important race and I decided my priorities were
in yachting.'

'Did your family approve?'

'Are you joking? It went down like a sinker on a
fishing line! Dad and Mum placed a lot of importance
on university education. I guess it had been their dream
for me. It wouldn't have been so bad if I hadn't enjoyed
the course.'

'What happened?' Corrie asked.

'There was a ding-dong family barney. I ended up
flatting, determined to show them I was not only going
to win that race, I was going to win an Olympic gold
medal for yachting.'

'Should I suspect a well-developed streak of stub-
bornness in your character?' She saw the smile flicker
on his face. 'How did you make a living?'

'With difficulty. I worked at another boat designer's
place for so many hours a week, then I had an evening
job as an aerobics and fitness instructor. That was
good, because it helped my own exercise programme. I
made enough to live on and I was able to spend most
of my time on the water.'

'And your parents?'

'There's an expression about a problem merely being
a challenge with several solutions. They saw I was
handling the situation. Mum started checking my times
and sometimes they'd take out their yacht to give me
an extra hard, long race. In return, I promised that if I
wasn't included in the Games nomination list I'd return
to varsity.'

'Did you ever regret it?' Corrie asked.

'Frequently! I was always broke—the yachts used to

need money more than salt water. Trying for the maximum, I'd break gear or I'd have to save for a new set of sails. And the girls I wanted to go out with would get seasick if I tried taking them out on the yacht. . .it wasn't till much later that I learnt to let them control the pace.'

'Are you telling me something?' she smiled.

'Perhaps.'

'You've got a wicked grin at times, Blake Hanley!' She thought it safer to change tack in the conversation. 'Your sister went to varsity?'

'Yes. She did accounting and later went into partnership with Dad. They're a pretty good team. Mum was very proud of her.'

Corrie saw the shadow on his face. Without saying anything she held his gaze.

'Yes, you're right,' he said. 'Mum died about a month after I won the Gold. A sudden illness, and then. . .'

'I'm sorry,' said Corrie softly.

'You lost your father, so I guess you know what it's like.' His hand covered hers on the tiller. For quite a long time they sat in harmony, letting the yacht sail towards the inlet. It was Corrie who spoke first.

'My parents showed me what a good marriage was all about. They were one of the few couples I knew who really loved each other. They'd discuss such wacky things,' she saw Blake's eyebrows raise, 'like, why the moon was made of Gruyere instead of vintage cheese, or why the seals had fur instead of feathers. I think communication with each other was a delight for both of them. They liked being together.'

'Your mother married again?'

'Yes. My stepfather is a good man, but I resented it at first. I was a polite pain! Fortunately my work took me away, and up in the mountains nature taught me not just to accept but to rejoice in my father's life.' She smiled, the tears close. A friendly arm slipped around her and Blake dropped a swift kiss on her mouth.

'You've been shaped by love for love, Corrie. I wish I could allow myself to fall in love with you.' His brown eyes searched hers. 'I'm sorry, Corrie.' He glanced away, and as they were sailing into the inlet he gestured her from the seat. 'I'd better take over, to swing in beside the jetty. Here's a boathook, can you grab one of the lines?'

The manoeuvre gave her the chance to compose her emotions so that when they were ready to climb ashore she was able to take Blake's hand and meet his eyes without showing the hurt. Together they carried the afternoon tea on to the shore of the inlet. It was a picture-postcard place; two old farmhouses, surrounded on three sides by the obligatory macrocarpa trees, watched over the inlet. The country road like a grey silk ribbon formed a bow joining the jetty to an empty parking and picnic area, then led back along the coast.

'It doesn't seem to have changed at all,' Blake commented as he looked around. 'Paul and I used to have races round to here and back. Yesterday he mentioned that the jetty had been repaired.'

'You must have been quite young,' said Corrie. 'Weren't you scared?'

'Regularly! But I liked to win, and as Paul had the same problem there was generally too much of a battle going on to worry about fear. Dad or Paul's parents had to be sailing within sight or we weren't allowed past the Heads.'

They walked towards a tree, and Corrie's eyes widened as she saw the picnic fare Blake produced. He unrolled a rug and patted the spot beside him. 'Sit down, Corrie, I don't want you to grow too good!'

The laughter in his eyes made him almost irresistible, Corrie decided, but for her own protection she had to enjoy his charm and not let his attraction affect her. With exaggerated care she selected a sandwich.

'Great!' She ate with enjoyment and reached for another. 'A man with imagination: asparagus and pastrami?'

'I'm a man of many talents.'

'And modest too,' she smiled. Diverting his attention, she passed him the plate of sandwiches. The flash of his white teeth as he took a deep bite was deliberately sensuous. It was an effort to pour the drink and try to appear calm knowing that Blake was enjoying watching her. When they had finished eating she packed up the remains of the picnic while Blake sprawled on the rug, his loose-limbed, lazy grace reminding her of a black panther. But she knew the panther was a dangerous creature. Was this the time to tell Blake about the photographs of the yacht? Mentally putting her facts in order, she drew a deep breath.

'Blake, earlier I took some photos of. . .'

With one hand he had picked up a gull's feather and was drawing it against her face, tickling her. Instinctively she bent, but he moved it to her ear and when she wriggled away he seized her feet, whipped off sneakers and socks and tormented her toes, reducing her to a laughing and pleading protest as he lay back and pulled her down beside him.

'You were frowning, and I couldn't allow that! I just knew you'd be ticklish, Corrie,' he murmured close to her ear. Corrie was held firmly. Her laughter faded as she felt his lips move along the line of her cheek, his eyes midnight-dark, until she could look at him no longer. Still breathless, she waited with trembling anticipation as he teased her mouth, enjoying his touch and his sensitivity. It was a long kiss, beginning like a wave, slowly but with complete certainty, growing and swelling until it crested and crashed.

Corrie struggled against his attraction. 'Someone might come along!' she protested.

'Come back here!' His voice was ragged and he thrust his left hand through his black hair in a gesture of frustration. 'Not a chance in a thousand.' He stroked her ear in an erotic gesture. 'Except perhaps a couple of magpies up in the trees, and they won't tell.'

With perfect timing a tourist bus appeared, heading inexorably towards them. Corrie's eyes met his and they both began chuckling.

'I give up! Let's get out of here!' Blake pushed her sneakers on to her feet, shoving her socks into her jacket pocket. He picked up the chilly-bin in one hand and reached for her with the other, and together they ran back to the trailer-sailer rocking gently at the jetty.

Releasing the yacht took only seconds, and with Blake at the tiller the craft sped out towards the sea. Corrie replaced the picnic bin in the cabin, then seeing her camera case she pulled out a lens, filters and camera. She had to keep away from Blake, and the camera would give her the excuse and perhaps the chance to talk photography and lead on naturally to the yacht photos. While they had been sailing she had noticed the water's ever-changing patterns, the sea foam white and emerald green, the angles of the mast and the halyards against the sky. . .and there was also the possibility of taking a photograph of Blake!

The angle of the yacht changed and she glanced towards the man at the tiller. He was concentrating as he changed tack, and she clicked the shutter as with one hand on the tiller he reached forward to adjust the sail. She climbed up to the deck and silently angling her camera began to take pictures of the curve of the sail, trying to capture the strength of the mast and the interplay of the sails. The water fascinated, and after some experiment she found that by lying out and along the side she could take a shot of the water creaming along the smooth hull of the yacht.

Blake's warning came a second too late to avoid the crest of a wave that sprayed over her. Blake grabbing her camera up and out of range just in time.

'You asked for that, Corrie!' he chuckled. 'A sailor's baptism!'

'You did it deliberately!' she snapped, accusing and indignant.

'Who me? Are you saying I control the waves?'

'Look at me—I'm soaked!'

'I'm looking!' he teased. He changed tack again and she made sure she was out of range as the boat nosed the water. 'There's a towel in the first cupboard and spare clothes in the second if you want to change. We'll be home in a few minutes.'

Surprised, Corrie glanced out as she towelled her face and hair. They had passed the headland and again Blake tacked to make a direct run to the entrance of Hidden Bay. She decided to wait till she was home to shower and change.

'Would you take her in while I get the sails down, Corrie?' he asked.

She nodded and stopped to take one more picture of him, relaxed and smiling at her, his expression sending her heartbeat racing again. Carefully she unscrewed the camera and put her gear away. Once up on deck she followed Blake's instructions as he pulled down the sails and wound up the centreboard. The sea had edged

along the beach, and the trailer, which had been high
and dry when they left, was now almost perfectly
positioned to take the boat. Blake jumped into the
water and eased it into place, then with the car hauled
it back into place beside the garage.

'Thank you for a wonderful afternoon, Blake,'
Corrie smiled. 'I felt I could sail with you forever.'

She saw the shutters close his expression and was
hurt, her happiness evaporating. How could she have
forgotten? Her imagination had been telling her he
cared for her, but she had been tricked by her own
sexuality. Heart aching, she bent and picked up the
camera bag and walked, shoulders hunched, sneakers
alternately squelching and squeaking, towards her own
vehicle. Wordless, Blake let her go.

At the farmhouse it didn't take her long to shower
and change. Not wanting to let her emotions spill out,
she deliberately began working in the studio, knowing
the process would numb the ache she felt. After
developing the day's film she sorted through the negatives with critical eyes.

The first was the snap of the yellow-eyed penguin
posing with a querying glance that charmed her. She
had been almost surprised to see it on the negative and
could only mock herself with the realisation she had
been so tormented by jealousy she had overlooked the
shot she had waited so many dawns to achieve. She
made a silent promise to herself that she would never
be jealous again.

The sea sequence she had taken was experimental,
and she would print them to assess further. The first
negative of Blake was worth enlarging, she decided;
the positioning of his body, the right angle formed with
his arm and his strong, scarred fingers on the tiller gave
the linear pattern she had sought, while the sky behind

him had given a neutral background. She put it down and flicked through the film to reach the last negative.

Aware of her lens, he had destroyed her usual thoughtful composition by smiling at her. The result was worse than an amateur's holiday snapshot. The background was poor, the yacht's rails sprouting from his arms, the halyards growing from his shoulders like some demented alien's antenna. In the limited light something about his expression held her. Puzzled, she decided to add it to the pile to print.

Two hours later she studied the photo again. She had put it in a frame and she was smiling. It had taken a lot of her time, a lot of fudging and fuzzing of the background to get rid of the rails and halyards, but it had been worth the effort! Blake was smiling, a smile full of tenderness, the warmth and humour in him revealed specially for her.

A man in love!

Hadn't she seen that same loving tenderness in his gaze when he had laughed with her as the camper-van had rolled into view? And when he had triumphantly tickled her into submission? Or was she making up some fantasy she wanted to make real?

Suddenly conscious of hunger, she left the studio and went along to the kitchen. Preparing pasta and vegetables was a prosaic task, but Philip was late home and he would be pleased if a meal was ready. The telephone rang and she answered it, her joy being crushed when it was not Blake. It was only when she was stirring the pasta that she remembered Blake had told Philip he had a prior engagement for the evening. She felt as limp as the spaghetti in the pot.

The indignant mew of one of the kittens alerted her to the fact that she had two hungry animals lined up.

'I'll feed you in a minute,' she promised as she finished setting the table.

Their vocabulary and volume increased, ceasing only when she stooped to feed them seconds before her brother arrived.

'You've had a good day!' Philip grinned chirpily. 'You forgot the mail!'

'And you have a letter from Misty!'

'Yes. The boys sent you a drawing each. Misty said one's an albatross and the other's a penguin. Abstract interpretation!'

Corrie held out her hands for the sheets he pulled from his pocket. 'This is Roddy, I'd know him anywhere!' she laughed as she viewed the boys' work. 'See the red identification rings on his leg?'

'Is that what you call it? Looks more like an apple tree to me! Artistic licence? Incidentally, I thought I might go up to Christchurch tomorrow,' Philip added. 'Can you hold the fort here for another couple of days?'

'Of course. Next week I've got the Fiordland series to continue. I'll be away ten days.'

'That's why I decided to go tomorrow,' he told her. 'The wedding's set for the seventh of next month.'

'The Seventh! That's three days after I get back from Fiordland!' Corrie exclaimed.

'I know. I checked your schedule against the minister's and the caterer's when I gave possible dates to Misty.'

'But nothing's been done!' she protested.

'No panic! Misty and I worked out a small list of guests, and Misty said she's finished the invitations and put them in the post. Our minister has agreed to the time, the licence has been prepared, the caterer will do the work—hey presto!'

Corrie began to laugh. 'I should have known! I'll be lucky to have time to find a dress.'

'I think this letter should be read first,' said Philip.

She picked up the envelope. 'It's from Misty?' She read the letter quickly, the neat, artistic writing familiar. 'She wants me to be bridesmaid—how lovely! She hopes I'll say yes, she's already seen the perfect dress for me—cream with a lining of sea-green! Trust Misty!'

'I do!' laughed Philip. He sobered. 'Misty had to learn to trust herself, that's why she left Taiaroa. I promised I'd give her time to prove she could manage alone. I knew she could do it, but it was a long wait. I'd have married her yesterday if we could have organised it in time!'

Corrie hugged him. 'I'm pleased it worked out. You deserve each other and the boys!' She went to the telephone. 'I'll ring her and accept straight away. You can bring the gown back with you. Then I'll have to ring the estate agents and tell them to find me a house.'

It was only when she was lying in bed that she was able to pull out the photo of Blake. His eyes, dark and full of love, met hers. It was just a trick of the camera, she told herself, but just for one night she was going to pretend that he loved her. After all, didn't she love him?

CHAPTER NINE

'WILL THOU Misty, have this man to thy wedded husband. . .love, honour and serve him. . .'

The familiar words had a solemnity dramatically emphasised by the background roll and wash of the sea. Corrie looked at her brother, and the love in his eyes as he gazed at his bride was matched by Misty's expression. Their love had grown like a seedling, strengthening with the small, ordinary daily changes, and now it could show itself proudly, blossoming like the starry flowers in Misty's boquet.

'I pronounce that they be man and wife together. . .'

The feeling of someone watching her made Corrie turn slightly, to see Blake sitting on the rocks. He had chosen his spot well, he could see the wedding party, but an outcrop protected him from being seen by the guests. Blake's smile sent her heart rhythm into fast time.

'You may kiss the bride.'

Blake raised his hand to his mouth and blew her a kiss. Since the morning of their sail she hadn't seen him, and the ache in her heart hardened into the pain of distrust. She had waited for him to ring or visit, and her misery had grown with the hours despite the flurry of activity before she departed for the trip to Fiordland.

Yet he sat smiling at her just as lovingly as in the photograph she had thrown into the waters of Milford Sound.

'Corrie, Corrie?' The whisper from the little boy

standing beside her drew her attention to the albatross gliding along the shore line. 'There's Roddy!'

'Shh!' his twin was loftily righteous. 'Mum and Dad——' he paused and his smile at the now official title went straight to Corrie's heart '——Mum and Dad are signing the book.'

Misty and Philip turned to hug the boys. Corrie handed over the bouquet, and kissed the bride and groom. When she looked again towards the rocks Blake was climbing back towards Hidden Bay. The ceremony officially over, she allowed the best man to escort her towards the lawn with its blue and white marquee.

Amid laughter and joy the photographs were taken, the reception passed in a happy haze, and in the evening the bride and groom departed, their car festooned with a trail of rattling cans and 'Just Married' signs. It was late when Corrie, her mother and stepfather said goodbye to the last guests.

'Everything went off very well!' her mother sighed. 'I thought the twins would never go to sleep!'

Her stepfather yawned. 'Those two are more active than fleas on a dog! I'm going to bed. It's exhausting becoming an instant grandfather.'

'It's a pity you can't stay on and help me with them,' said his wife.

'Agreed, but our business really needs either your mother or me, and preferably both of us. And we do enjoy working together.' His smile for his wife made his love obvious. 'Everyone off to bed? I'll switch the lights off.'

Corrie had intended to walk on the beach, but she followed them upstairs. She was tired, and her emotions of the day had run the gamut from happiness to near-despair. In her bedroom she went to shut the window, but the call of an albatross in distress surprised her. Standing still, she listened as it cried again, close by the bridal blossoming of the plum tree.

Blake was leaning against the trunk of the tree! Hands slightly cupped over his mouth, he gave the albatross call again, softer, as though more distant. The sound was a near-perfect imitation. He gestured Corrie down, and after a moment's indecision she picked up her jacket, slipped down the stairs and out into the garden, her pace slowing as she walked towards him, already regretting her action.

'I knew you wouldn't be able to resist an albatross in trouble, Corrie.' His voice was even more sensuous than memory had replayed in her mind.

'Call it curiosity,' she said. 'I'm wondering why you bothered.'

'I don't deserve that!'

'You're feeling neglected?' Corrie pulled on her jacket, punching her arms into the sleeves. 'I wonder why? Could it have anything to do with the fact that you gave me one of the most incredible mornings of my life and then didn't bother to contact me?'

'You didn't tell me you were off to the wilderness,' Blake told her.

'It was a routine visit. I was home for three days before I left. Do you know how long that was?'

'Every minute of it. I wanted you. I thought if I kept my distance and kept busy. . .it didn't work. When I admitted defeat and rang you Philip told me you'd left an hour earlier. To go to the Takahe Valley!' Blake leaned forward and took her arm. 'In the Murchison mountains, the middle of nowhere! Total isolation, no telephone, no roads! How could you do that? Don't you realise what a risk you took—out there, all alone?'

'There are no lions or tigers or snakes in the New

Zealand bush. Unfortunately for photographers, rare birds don't make a habit of living near hotels.'

'Don't be clever with me, Corrie, I'm not in the mood! I've had days of sheer hell wondering if I'd ever see you alive again! According to the weather office Fiordland had thunder, lightning and heavy rain for six days. And you were backpacking!'

'Such concern!' shrugged Corrie. 'I might believe you if you'd bothered to meet me when I arrived home. You didn't even ring!'

'Is that what you think? You were due back at six on Monday night. I rang every half-hour until Philip got so fed up and promised to ring me when you arrived. I spent the night wondering where the hell you were. As far as I knew you could have been missing for a week! I was haunted by the thought of your having fallen and lying injured.'

Corrie looked at him and a small light of hope dared to glow. It didn't mean more than concern, she reminded herself, but even that was a ray of love to be appreciated, wasn't it?

'Corrie, when you still hadn't arrived by six the next morning I drove over here to demand that Philip call out a search party,' Blake told her.

'You didn't!' Corrie's eyes sparkled with humour. 'Philip would have loved you!'

'I'd hardly slept for eight nights worrying about you, and there he was sleeping like a contented pig!' he added.

Corrie could not stop a chuckle. 'Poor Philip!'

'Poor Philip? Don't you mean poor Blake? Only then did he tell me that you used a radio to check into Park headquarters on a regular basis and that if you missed a call he would have been notified immediately. Only then did he tell me you'd done a specialised radio course. And only then did he discover that, given extreme provocation, I can lose my temper!'

'I'm sorry you were alarmed.' Corrie's apology was split with laughter. Softening, she decided to explain. 'Before I could get out I had to cross what's usually a small creek. With the rain it had turned into a white water torrent, so I had to sit and wait three days until I could cross safely—it happens quite often in the mountains. In the end I had to radio for the helicopter pilot to fly in and pick me up. Did Philip tell you I rang from Milford Sound?'

'Yes.' His smile showed a flash of white teeth. 'He has a strong will to live. But all he could tell me was that you'd sounded exhausted and intended sleeping.'

'I was tired, and the thought of driving back was too much. I went to bed and caught the early morning plane out. It put me back in Dunedin in time for morning tea with Misty and the boys. One of my ranger friends will bring my car back.'

'I rang late afternoon and Philip told me you were in the city,' said Blake. 'Then you were booked for the rehearsal with the family. He suggested I talk to you at the wedding.'

'But you just watched from the rocks. After that you didn't bother!' Corrie protested.

'Philip had shown me the guest list, several I knew well. I hoped to see you on your own, but. . .'

'You wanted to see me?' She was behaving like the kittens, hungry for love.

'What do you think?' Corrie quivered at the low timbre of his voice. 'Have you any idea how beautiful you are, in that dress? Like sea-foam, so delicate you might float off into space.' His self-mocking smile at his lyricism was tender. 'You should be swooning in my arms by now.'

'I never swoon,' she admitted breathlessly. 'Perhaps if you kiss me——?'

His mouth was a moth-light touch on her upturned lips. Corrie put her arms around him and felt the hard solidity of his backbone as she leaned against the warmth of his chest. She could hear the speeding thud of his heart. The faint smell of quality male cologne and a clean shirt intermingled teasingly with the slight musk tones of his body. His mouth nuzzled her ear and she shivered with pleasure, his breath a warm touch on her nape. He was drawing out the moment, tantalising her lips, with brief touches, his hands playing songs on her skin. His kiss claimed her, the deep of his mouth exciting the instant flare of passion; and Corrie melted against him, unable to resist the sensuous magic. Until she realised he was kissing her as if he loved her. She pulled away, trembling, but he gentled her back into the nest of his body. 'Why, Corrie?' His voice was soft against her hair. It took all her courage to answer.

'Please, Blake, don't pretend! I couldn't bear it.'

'I'm not pretending. I never have pretended with anyone, and I don't intend to start with the woman I love, my stormy petrel!' He kissed her again, decisive and strong in his movements, his mouth a love song against hers. 'I love you Corrie!' It was a dedication, his voice low and rich, his midnight gaze steady. 'When you were away I was forced to admit how much you meant to me. I would admit to wanting you, needing you, admiring you, and after several days I could even face the fact that I could be just a little in love with you. . .' He stopped to drop light kisses on her hair. 'Today, on the beach, at the wedding I realised the truth. When I saw you, I knew I loved you. While I was coming to terms with the idea, you looked at me and I knew you were the woman I had to marry.' His

fingers traced the outline of her face and he smiled with
engaging tenderness. 'Corrie, it was a shock! You know
how I felt about marriage, or should I say, how I used
to think about it. I scarpered off the rocks as though a
tsunami was due!'

Her body trembled, she wanted to believe him, but
her enforced isolation had given her time to think.
'Maybe it was just the romance of the situation, Blake,'
she said quietly.

'I told myself that too. But I've been to weddings
before and rarely felt anything more than a mild, lustful
cynicism for the bridesmaids. Believe me, there's absol-
utely nothing mild about the lustful feelings I have for
you.' He kissed her, his passion aroused as soon as
their lips met. 'You knocked me off my feet when we
first met and I've been reeling from the impact ever
since.' He caressed the contour of her head, smoothing
a few curls into place. 'I convinced myself that my
monastic lifestyle was to blame and that if I had a few
nights with you the fever would leave me.'

It was a thought which had already plagued Corrie.
'It's possible,' she agreed.

'Don't think you can get out of it so easily, my love,'
said Blake. 'I want to be with you in twenty and thirty
years' time. By that time I might begin to understand
you. I might even be able to work out how you fascinate
me.' He kissed a curl. 'But like our albatross friends
I'm yours for life.' He turned her so he could see her
face in the moonlight.

Eyes wide, she looked at him, knowing she could
believe him. His kisses had been full of love, echoing
his claim. In his eyes she could read its shining message,
her sensitivity could feel it in his touch; his honesty had
forced him to admit the truth. He loved her!

'At the wedding you were standing beside the twins,'

he went on. 'It struck me what a caring, loving mother you would be, then the best man walked towards you and I felt outraged! I intend to father your children.' His kiss was swift, proprietorial. 'I've never even thought about raising a family before! That's when I knew our course was charted and set.'

'Do I have a say?' Corrie looked at him with shining eyes.

'You can say you love me.'

'Blake, I love you.' She said the words, then leaned forward to kiss him, her lips warm and full and moist, brushing against the hard line of his jaw and the faint prickle of his shaven skin until she reached his lips. She felt the quick response, the surging rush of joy as he let her mouth nestle against his.

'Corrie. . .my love. . .' His voice was so low she could barely make out the words he was murmuring against her skin. He kissed her in a triumphant demanding, glorying passion, whirling her into a dizzying cloud of sensation, until the night seemed to grow dark around her and she was floating in ecstasy.

'Corrie, my little bird, my petrel. . .'

She opened her eyes. Blake was holding her, his expression one of tender resolve.

'I must let you go, my darling. It's after midnight, a new day. You must be tired, and we've all the time in the world ahead of us.' Taking her hand, he kissed the back of her wrist and then walked beside her to the door.

'Goodnight, Blake.' She caressed the side of his face with her hand. 'I'm almost afraid to go. In the morning I'm scared I'll wake up and find tonight has been a dream.'

She felt his kiss of reassurance.

'Corrie, I'll love you as long as there's wind in the air and water in the ocean and the sun in the sky.'

Faint noises of the household having breakfast disturbed Corrie in the morning. She turned over, determined to snuggle down and catch up on lost sleep, then remembered her miracle. Blake loved her! A sunbeam glinting through the upper leadlight window shot a rainbow of colours on to the wall. The sun was in the sky. . . Blake loved her!

Showered and dressed, she ran downstairs in a mood of eager happiness. The chorus of greeting warmed her.

'Corrie—good morning, darling! You look wonderful after your sleep.' Her mother kissed her.

'Congratulations, Corrie!'

Corrie looked puzzled, then realised her stepfather was holding out the morning's paper.

'You won, darling!' her mother smiled. 'What a magnificent photo!'

'Congratulations, Corrie—you've scooped the pool!' Her stepfather adjusted his bifocals and began to read. '"The National Awards for Photography were announced in Auckland last evening. Dunedin's international wildlife photographer, Miss Corrie Seton, submitted three entries to achieve four gold awards, winning the Action category, the Romance category, the Nature section and——"' he paused for dramatic effect '"—winner of the Best Overall Entry, for her action study of a racing yacht!"'

'Corrie, listen to this!' Her mother read over his shoulder, '"The chief judge comments that the winning entry is artistically composed, shows excellent use of natural light, and complete mastery of techniques.

'Miss Seton,' said the judge, 'demonstrated that her abilities cover all the vision of the camera'."'

Corrie could only gaze in horror. Her photo of the racing yacht had been reprinted in full colour by the local paper and occupied half the front page!

'And on the Otago page, they've printed your other two shots,' her mother said proudly. 'See the article? "Well done, C. S.! Our regular nature photographer C. S., Corrie Seton, has not only been recognised as. . ." Corrie, are you all right? You look white.'

'Shock! Sit down.' Her stepfather pulled out a chair and poured her a cup of tea. 'When did you see Blake Hanley's new yacht, Corrie?'

'How do you know it's Blake's?' she croaked to her stepfather.

'Well, it has to be, doesn't it? I can't see the faces, but I bet that's Paul Greywood. He's wearing an Otago rugby shirt and you can see the number seven, his position, and everyone knows he's Blake's friend as well as lawyer—the two of them used to sail cats in Hidden Bay. He's a top-line sailor. This one, the navigator with his head bent over the laptop computer, has been with Blake for years. I'd know him anywhere. I'm fairly certain that's Blake at the helm, half hidden by the mast.' His fingers went from pointing to the figures to caressing the line of the yacht. 'Besides, the paper agrees with me.' He read aloud, '"Mystery yacht subject of gold-winning photo. A sea trial of a new yacht in Corrie Seton's photo has caused immediate speculation. It is known that Ms Seton has recently returned from the isolated coastline of the Gulf of Carpentaria in Australia. When we tried to contact Ms Seton last night the Taiaroa photographer could not be reached. Is it an Australian challenger for the Round the World Race? Or is it New Zealand's own Blake

Hanley's latest winner? We believe the latter. One crew member, partially obscured, is wearing an Otago rugby jersey. The game is now on to find the yacht!"'

Her stepfather looked at Corrie, sudden inspiration lighting his face, then he flicked back to the second page. 'It's just outside! That's it, again, with the morning sea mist off the nursery headland. He's keeping it in Hidden Bay!'

Corrie sat numbed. If her sports-mad stepfather could piece together the evidence so easily. . .she couldn't allow her thoughts rein.

'I'm right—you've been sworn to secrecy!' he persisted. 'The boatshed! I bet it's in the old boatshed!'

'If Corrie had been sworn to secrecy she would hardly have sent these photos forward,' her mother intervened, then turned to her husband. 'Didn't you say you wanted to leave early? If you're going to pack the car perhaps the twins could help you.' Her mother smiled and blew her husband a kiss as he regretfully put down the paper and departed followed by his eager helpers. 'Corrie, drink your tea and eat something. There are a pile of congratulatory messages I've been taking for you. The telephone's been busy. Someone left it off the hook last night, so no one could contact you then. It's possibly just as well, judging by the calls. There were several from the sports departments of the newspapers and a couple from radio and television. One was from Paul Greywood—he was quite insistent about speaking to you. I had the impression he hadn't rung to congratulate you.'

'He wouldn't,' Corrie admitted miserably. 'I thought the competition entries had been withdrawn. I rang the secretary when I found out how important they were to Blake.'

'Do you want to come up with us to Christchurch for

a few days? Or should I stay with you?' asked her mother.

'No, thanks, Mum. I made the mistake, I'll handle it. Besides, I'm entrusted with the twins. Can you keep them here while I talk to Blake?'

Ten minutes later Corrie dropped from the rocks into Hidden Bay. Blake was chopping wood, and the steady, relentless action of axe and shoulders caught at her heart. She could remember her father chopping wood when he was angry. It seemed to take her a long time to cross the sand, the sound of each stroke matching her footsteps. When she stood opposite him he stopped and put the axe down with deliberate care.

'Blake, I'm sorry,' she said quietly.

'You, sorry? You won, didn't you? All the prestige, the prize money! I hope you think it was worth it!'

She had seen trapped, injured animals before, their gaze a composite of suffering, anguish and hate. But when Blake looked at her she felt as if she had seen his soul.

He bent, picked up a piece of wood and threw it towards the pile. When he straightened, he was back in control, his eyes hooded.

'Just go, Corrie!' he said shortly.

'I came to see you because I know what you must be thinking! Blake, I love you!'

'You love me?' His laugh was sour, bitter. 'Corrie, your actions have shown me your real feelings, your real values.' He began to walk back to the cottage, but Corrie stood her ground.

'At least listen to my explanation!' she begged. A dozen times I was going to tell you I'd already taken a film of *Taiaroa's Petrel* the first day I saw it. I didn't realise there was anything secret about the yacht—I just thought it looked beautiful. It didn't enter my head to ask you for permission when I sent in the entry for the competition. . .' She was speaking to a solid door.

Blake had walked out of her life.

For a minute she turned and gazed at the sea, trying to forget the look of anguish in his eyes, knowing he was going through pain he could not shut out. If he had not loved her and believed himself loved the betrayal would have angered him, but it would not have hurt him. Like a wounded animal, he had dragged himself away to hide.

Her mother was waiting on the beach when Corrie crossed back along the rocks.

'He didn't listen?' her mother asked. 'Give him time. He probably only found out himself in the last hour. If he still doesn't want to listen, write to him.'

Corrie could only nod. The arrival of the twins, squealing with excited laughter as they chased the kittens, forced her to put away her own feelings. Fifteen minutes later, she stood, a twin on either side, and waved a farewell.

The telephone ringing sent both of them racing to answer, but handing over the receiver, they informed her excitedly that it was from New York.

'Miss Seton? It's *Yachtsman World*. The pic has just been faxed to us in New York. Congratulations! Looks like Hanley has a real winner there! We'd like to commission you to send us a photo essay on the yacht.'

The trap was set. If she confirmed or denied she was in trouble.

She spoke with secretarial efficiency. 'I'm sorry, I can't help you at the moment. If you write to Ms Seton with your request and your terms she should be back from Fiordland by the time your letter arrives.'

She put down the telephone quickly, then lifted it off the hook. Only the boys' dismay reminded her that they were waiting for their own call, and she replaced it. 'OK, let's tidy up the kitchen, and after that we'll go down to the beach,' she said.

She had barely moved away when the telephone buzzed again. The boys' chatter was reassuring. In turn she spoke to Philip and Misty, and their happiness mocked her own misery. When they had finished talking she unplugged the phone.

'Corrie, can we take a picnic down to the beach?' asked one twin.

'There's heaps of food,' added the second.

'Good idea!' she smiled.

They were sorting out the crayfish and chicken delicacies when the arrival of the caterers' men to take down the marquee reminded her that the road gate had been unlocked the previous day. The boys forgot the picnic and the kittens in their interested observation, as the big tent was taken down and the rest of the caterers' equipment stacked in the van.

'We can wave the men goodbye from the gate,' Corrie suggested a short time later. The boys were happy to swing the big gate shut, but their eyes opened wider when they saw the chain. As she fastened the lock in place Corrie realised that if reporters did travel to the farm it would be easy enough to walk to the farmhouse and finding it deserted look to the beach. It was just too close! Sooner or later she would have to face the reporters and messages, but she needed more time.

'What do you say to a fishing picnic on the boat?' she asked the boys.

Their ecstatic faces were the answer.

'I'll get the keys!'

'Race you!'

Half an hour later Corrie throttled the motor and

they began gliding through the water, the boys taking turns being skipper or chief seaweed spotter until they reached almost the end of the protective headland. She could see the farmhouse, but she was far enough away to be unrecognisable.

'Cut the motor!' she ordered.

She lowered the anchor while the boys pulled out the fishing gear, left untouched since their last expedition with Philip. They chattered like sparrows as they baited the hooks, bemoaning the fact that they hadn't had enough time to dig for many plump earthworms. The sea was quiet, with barely a ripple to rock the boat. Watching the boys casting and recasting, Corrie decided she was quite safe from the possibility of them ever catching a fish.

Before she left the house she had put the mail and the morning's messages into a bag. The messages were mostly congratulatory, many with requests to contact back. Corrie noted her friends and then summarised the media list. She was left with Paul Greywood's name and three advertising agencies. Paul's was a call she would have to answer, the rest would have to wait. The boys were energetically throwing their lines out, so she reached for her mail. There was quite a large stack, having built up over the time she had been away in Fiordland. Riffling through it, she stopped at the distinctive logo of the Society of Photographers. She opened it and read the letter.

Dear Ms Seton,

At the last meeting of the Society's Awards Committee your request to withdraw your entries in the Romance and Action categories was tabled.

One of the committee suggested that as the prestige and prize money is considerable your unusual request might not have been bona fide. The President has instructed me to ask you to verify your request in writing.

This must be done by return mail or fax in order to meet our time limit.

The neat businesslike signature of the secretary was familiar. Corrie sighed. The postmark showed that it had been sent well before she left for Fiordland. If she had not been away. . .if she could have warned Blake. . .if she had not won! She could not accept the prize money. A pair of shags flew low over the water as she pondered what to do with it. The Wildlife Centre was an obvious answer.

'Two people are walking towards the beach,' one of the boys commented as he played with her binoculars.

'Do we have to go back? We've only been out a little while.'

'Not yet. You haven't caught any fish for dinner. Let me check, then we'll have our picnic soon.' Corrie took the binoculars and focused on the figures on shore. She recognised the sports editor and one of the photographers of the local paper. They had given up the telephone! She was glad of the extra power of the binoculars. Without a specialist distance lens the photographer would not be able to make out more than the fact that two or three were fishing. To make sure she pulled on her brother's fishing hat and his sunglasses, much to the delight of the boys, convinced she was being comical for their benefit. She was not so sure of her plan when she observed another couple arrive at the farmhouse. They left their equipment there, then walked down to the beach to join the returning sports editor and photographer. It looked as if a discussion was taking place, and when a larger group arrived shortly afterwards with television cameras Corrie began to feel trapped.

'I'm hungry!' complained James.

'I don't think there are any fish in this sea today!' Matthew said as he hauled in a lump of seaweed. 'We usually catch heaps!'

'Never mind. Try again later. Wipe your hands and we'll have lunch,' said Corrie with a bright smile stitched on to her face.

She was relieved when after their meal both boys settled on to the foam seats and although still holding their rods, drifted off to sleep, looking rather like misplaced garden gnomes. She adjusted the awning to shade them, then began reading the rest of her mail. From time to time she checked the knot of people who had moved from the beach back to the farmhouse. Apart from noticing that as someone arrived others left, she made notes about her correspondence on the backs of the letters. The boys slept on, and she began to worry that the group would still be waiting when she had to return.

The appearance of a small yacht was of only mild interest until she realised its tack would be in a direct course with her boat. Reaching for the binoculars, she checked the figure at the tiller, relaxing when one glance told her it was not Blake. A second look made her frown. It was Paul Greywood, and he didn't look as if he was out for a pleasant afternoon's sail. Within a few minutes he had cruised to a stop alongside.

'You didn't reply to my message, Corrie.'

'I haven't replied to any. Once I realised how much the pictures meant to Blake I asked for them to be withdrawn. I thought they had been.' Her voice cracked. 'Blake's so hurt.' She brushed away the tears which had sprung from nowhere. 'I'm sorry.' She blew her nose and looked away for a moment to regain control.

'I was all set to blow you to pieces, but you're as upset as Blake.' Paul sighed. 'Maybe I should have warned him when I received the portrait you sent me, but I was afraid it would destroy any chance of a relationship between you. Instead I tried to contact you. Philip told me you'd gone to Fiordland and couldn't be reached.'

'I got this letter this morning, it should have reached me before I went to Fiordland, but. . .' Corrie handed over the letter from the secretary, and Paul skimmed through it.

'I'd like to show it to Blake.'

'If you think it would help him, take it. I'll donate the prize money to the Taiaroa Wildlife Centre,' Corrie told him.

'That's generous of you.'

'I can't keep it, it would be too much like thirty pieces of silver.'

'The odds were against you,' Paul told her. 'Just after the Olympics, Blake was interested in a young photographer; she took photos of his friends at a party and sold the shots to a tabloid for a mint.'

Corrie felt sick. 'I wondered. There's nothing I can do to minimise the damage?' she asked.

'If you could avoid confirmation for two days we'll take advantage of the speculation and publicity around and announce that Blake will sail the *Petrel* in at midday on the third day—we haven't a hope of keeping the media at bay any longer.'

'I can't avoid going home,' Corrie told him. 'I have the twins, as well as keeping an eye on the farm and feeding the dogs and letting them off for a run. But if I can help I will.'

Paul nodded. 'Think you can avoid giving away the fact that Blake's living at Hidden Bay?'

'I won't tell anyone. How did you know where to find me?'

'Blake saw you from the top of the cliff. He told me the farmhouse had been kept under observation. I'd better push off before someone guesses.'

Paul pulled the jib sheet taut and the little craft sped away, leaving Corrie alone with her thoughts and the sleeping twins. The excitement of the previous days must have been too much, as they continued to sleep for another half an hour. Most of the media gave up, leaving only a trio on guard. Reluctantly Corrie headed the boat back towards Beach Farm.

As she approached shore she saw the photographer set up his gear, so, feeling rather like the hunted quarry, she waved a greeting. She knew all three slightly, the photographer, a junior reporter and the third a radio journalist who specialised in current affairs.

'Congratulations, Corrie!' they called.

'Thank you! It's nice of you to come out to congratulate me.'

'What can you tell us about the boat?'

'Help me winch it up and I'll give you as much detail as I can, but I know next to nothing about them. I'm quite willing to talk photography. On the subject of animals, I can be a bore!'

The speed the boat was put to bed left Corrie no illusions that they meant business.

'Just how fast can it go?' asked the reporter.

'It depends on the sea, the currents and of course, the wind.'

'But what speed?'

'I don't know, I've never had it flat out!'

Their laughter and the sight of their scribbling pencils and the steady revolutions of the tape recording reassured her.

'Who designed it?'

Corrie named a well-known Auckland designer who had designed the runabout.

'Where did you take your photograph?'

'I take photographs all over the world,' she explained. 'If you're talking about the boat, I first photographed it near Picton.'

'That's logical, there are plenty of bays to hide a yacht.'

'What was the name of the bay?' the radio journalist checked.

'Look, I'm sorry, I wouldn't have a clue,' said Corrie. 'We went there by seaplane because there were no roads. Glorious spot—bush-covered hills down to the waterline and the house and boatshed almost invisible, blending with the trees.

'You were invited there?' asked the reporter.

'Yes, of course.'

'Do you know any of the dimensions? Length? Width? What she draws?'

'Sorry, you're asking the wrong person. She's quite beamy. Stability is important. For the fishing, you understand!' Corrie risked a smile.

'Fishing?' The reporter looked dismayed. 'What do you say on the subject of Blake Hanley?'

'Nothing at all! I'm quite prepared to discuss my work, but I would be unwise to discuss others',' Corrie said firmly.

'Is it Hanley's yacht? In the award photo?'

A tugging, an anxious, silent plea and a cross-legged stance from one of the boys, made Corrie smile. 'Sorry, you can see we've got an urgent call to make!'

She ran with the boys up to the house. As she noticed the trio head back to the gate she wondered when they would realise she had been speaking about Philip's runabout. With the boys, kittens and guilt at her heels she raced through the chores, then replugged the phone. It started ringing before she stood up. A dozen phone calls later she had her 'Unavailable' comment down to a few words, deciding that the less said, the better. The boys' excited yells that she was on the television news dismayed her. Footage taken when she was named as one of the top ten international wildlife photographers showed her walking along Farm Beach, enthusiastic and happy. The item showed her gold medal winning shots, they stayed with the action shot of the yacht to add an interview with a yachting reporter who commented that the yacht had several features, including the positioning, size, height and make-up of the mast, the width of the working deck area and the cut of the sails. He agreed that it was almost certainly Blake Hanley's and with a smile challenged Blake, wherever he was, to show the yacht.

Corrie, her mouth dry, winced. Such a knowledgeable reporter on seeing the earlier footage of her at Farm Beach might make a point of checking on its location. If he knew Blake's childhood home was on the Otago Peninsula, how long would it be before the secret of Hidden Bay was exposed? How much more damage could she cause the man she loved? Was Blake wondering the same thing?

CHAPTER TEN

BY THE time the boys were ready for their bedtime story the constantly ringing telephone with calls from news services, international television and radio had made Corrie decide they would have to leave the house early in the morning. The boys eagerly suggested a trip to the city to go swimming at the heated pool, followed by a movie. She kissed them goodnight after promising to check the paper for details.

As she went downstairs she remembered that her car was still at Milford Sound. The telephone ringing again seemed to mock her. It was hard assuming a bright voice and taking down yet another offer for more studies of the yacht. The prices were growing with the speculation. Slowly she walked along to her studio and put on the light. Her filing system had to be good, and it was only a minute before she picked out the file of the yacht studies and walked back to the living-room. The pictures of Blake and the crew were bright and clear, and judging by the persistent phone calls, of considerable value. Thoughtfully Corrie picked up the telephone and dialled Paul Greywood's number. An answerphone informed her that Paul was unavailable and would respond to a message in due course. She gritted her teeth and wished she had a similar machine, then bent and pulled the plug on the telephone, deciding she needed some peace.

In the dawn she packed items needed for the day and threw a bag into the truck before going to wake the boys. Together they did the chores, then drove round

the farm, the twins opening and shutting gates and
arguing about their turns in their high-pitched voices.

'Look, Corrie, there's a television van coming along
our road!'

'It's not. Yes, it is! It's stopping at our gate!'

'Perhaps it just wants to turn around in our driveway,' Corrie answered the boys, and swung the truck
into the next paddock. In her rear-vision mirror she
saw the van stop at the farm road, but she continued
her drive along the farm track until another gate
allowed them to cross their neighbour's fields and from
there join a metalled back road which led to the clifftop
route back to the city.

'We'll have breakfast in town,' she smiled, seeing the
puzzled look on the boys' faces.

'Can we have pancakes?'

'With lemon and golden syrup?'

She managed to nod. The lump in her throat eased
as she drove along the peninsula. The boys were
unaware of her hurt as they chattered on, identifying
the distinctive hills like old friends.

In town Corrie stopped outside the legal office where
Paul Greywood worked, and the open door encouraged
her. In the foyer she looked around, suddenly
uncertain.

'Miss Seton? Were you looking for Mr Greywood?
He's in his office, I'll see if he's available,' the receptionist smiled.

A box of toys lured the twins to investigate in the
corner, and the receptionist promised to keep watch on
them when she showed Corrie into a pleasant, sunlit
room. Two men were standing beside the window, and
Corrie felt her heart skip a beat.

'Good morning, Corrie.' Paul moved to point her to
a chair, but Blake remained quiet, a slight inclination

of his head and his implacable gaze indicating his
hostility.

'No, I have the twins with me. I brought these
negatives and photographs of Blake, the crew and the
yacht. Judging by these offers I've had they're of value,'
Corrie said.

'You're giving away the rights to them?' Blake
moved forward and took the photos and the list of
offers from her, taking care not to touch her hands.

'Yes.'

'Paul, will you get that statement in writing?' Blake
asked, and Paul nodded and left the room. Blake pulled
out the photos and spread them out on the desk. Corrie
felt despondent as he studied the pictures. A muscle
flicked in his cheek as he glanced at his own portrait,
but he said nothing, moving on to check the negatives
in the second envelope.

Paul came back into the room. 'One statement typed
for you to sign, Corrie.'

A staff member witnessed her signature, then
departed, promising to return with photo-copies.

Paul glanced at the photos on the desk. 'That's the
best portrait of you I've seen, Blake. Corrie, you're a
genius with a camera!' He smiled. 'Did Blake mention
that we heard a couple of comments from you about a
place in the Sounds on the local radio last night? It
sounded so sincere!'

'Corrie has a gift for sincerity!' Blake said
sardonically.

It was like a blow in the face. Corrie gasped with the
pain, then, not wanting Blake to see he had hurt her,
she walked from the room.

'Are we going to have pancakes now?' James abandoned the toys.

'We're starving, Corrie!' Matthew echoed.

'Pan-cakes, pan-cakes, pan-cakes!' The boys' sing-song chant, a syllable to each step, acted like a taunting reminder to Corrie. Seeing Blake had been a shock. She had been ripped apart by the expression in his dark eyes. He was controlled, quiet, authoritative, but the gentleness and humour and warmth in him had been scoured out, leaving him as hard and dangerous as the rocks in Hidden Bay.

During the long day her own feelings were held together by the band-aids of the twins' love and needs. Night was falling as they drove back to the farm in the truck, Matthew falling asleep first and his brother, afraid to be left out of anything, even his dreams, curling up beside him. Realising the local news would be on the radio, Corrie switched it on to a low level, but the sound of Blake's voice made her pull over to listen.

'. . .so tomorrow at noon we'll sail *Taiaroa's Petrel* down the Otago Harbour to the city.'

'Is it the yacht in Corrie Seton's gold medal photograph?'

'You'll be able to see at midday.'

The announcer said the interview had been recorded at a press conference earlier and went on to the next news item. Corrie's shoulders dropped as she relaxed, thankful the media would not be waiting for her at the famrhouse. Fifteen minutes later she unlocked the doors, switched on the lights, then carried first one warm, faintly chlorine-smelling, cuddly child up to the bedroom and then the second.

On the porch the kittens looked up from their box, stretched themselves, then began yowling in rising crescendo until she shifted them inside and filled their dishes. A chilly draught made her shiver and she walked into the studio to close the window. Hundreds of photographs littered the floor and her work table. Stunned, Corrie, eyes wide, looked round in dismay. The cabinet where she filed her work had been pulled away from the wall, and the contents emptied, drawers yawning open. It looked as if handfuls of her prints had been grabbed, flicked through and discarded, to lie wherever they dropped.

Dazed, she picked up an isolated, crumpled photograph of the wounded Roddy from the floor beside the door, her hands smoothing it as she tried to comprehend. The photograph was ruined. Her negatives! The sturdy second cabinet seemed intact. The negatives were filed in chronological order, dates printed on the drawers and inside, each folder was top listed with a reference number matched to a subject catalogue. The previous night she had ruled through an entry in red and closed her catalogue with the ruler at the same page. The catalogue had been opened and she guessed the scored entry had been read. She opened the latest drawer and the empty file marked 'Yacht. C/- P. Greywood, Solicitor' was fractionally higher than the rest, as though someone had pulled it out, checked that the file was empty and replaced it.

Shaken, she walked back to the kitchen and dialled Paul Greywood's number. He answered almost immediately.

'Paul, it's Corrie Seton. I'm sorry, I may have given you a problem. My studio. . .' her voice choked and she had to draw a breath to steady it, 'my studio in our house has been burgled and all the photos thrown everywhere. It will take days for me to check if any are missing, but I believe someone was after the yacht photos.'

'You're all right yourself, Corrie?' he asked in concern.

'Yes, we've just arrived home. I'll have to ring the police.'

'I'll do it. They'll take a while to reach you, though.'

'Paul, the burglar knows you have the yacht series. I wrote it in my negative file and book and I found the catalogue open on top of the cabinet. It's the only negative file they inspected, probably just to make sure the whole film had gone. If they. . .'

'Don't worry, Corrie, the photos have already been farmed out to a couple of studios,' said Paul. They're being reprinted at this moment. Blake's giving three of your pics in each of the media kits tomorrow and using the contacts on the list you gave us an agent's negotiating exclusive deals for the rest.'

'That's a relief! But the thief might visit your place tonight. . .'

'I rather wish he would, I've got half the crew here! Seriously, Corrie, take care. I'll ring the police now. Goodnight.'

Corrie put down the phone and, aware of her isolation, locked the kitchen door, checked that the rest of the windows and doors were secured, then on a sudden, terrifying thought ran to check that Matthew and James were still safe. She gave a noisy sigh of relief as she saw them snuggled up, sound asleep.

The sound of a car made her run to the window of the boys' room, memory plaguing her with the fact that she had not bothered to padlock the gate in the dark. The car was not one she knew, but when it stopped Blake's figure was instantly recognisable. Her instinct was to race down the stairs, throw herself at him and, weeping and wailing, admit to being a fragile woman needing comfort. By the time she had reached the landing she had remembered his earlier attitude and

taken several deep breaths so she would appear un-
ruffled and controlled.

'Good evening, Corrie.' His dark eyes inspected her.
'Paul rang me. The police are coming, but I thought I'd
check the place.'

'Thank you.'

Corrie watched as he methodically worked his way
through the house, checking cupboards and under
beds, thrusting curtains aside to ensure that the bay
windows were not hiding-places.

'This latch is broken, he's jemmied it open here.'
Blake pointed to a window in the studio.

'I thought I'd left everything secure,' said Corrie. 'I'll
get some wire to tie it in place for the night.'

'Don't touch it until the police have been,' he
advised.

She nodded, feeling brittle at the cold depths of his
voice. After putting the wire and pliers on the kitchen
bench she filled the kettle, a temporary, mind-numbing
action. Blake had gone out to his car, but he returned
with a kitbag.

'A sleeping bag?' Corrie queried.

'Yes, I'll stay the night, you and the boys are too
vulnerable.'

'Really, there's no need. I'm perfectly capable. . .'

'No,' he was uncompromisingly. Corrie gave in. It
would be easier to shift granite.

'Corrie, others could try, thinking the photographs
easy pickings. The combination of your photographic
skill and the mystery of the yacht created a valuable
demand. An agent has negotiated deals worth nearly
eighty thousand dollars in Europe and Japan, and one
exclusive photo essay in the North American market is
going to be worth half that again.' His lips tightened.
'Enough to tempt a burglar or two.' The thud of his

sleeping bag being fired on to the colonial couch along one wall of the kitchen was reassuring. 'You could be interested to know that the agent will be crediting your bank account with half. The other half will be split between the Taiaroa Wildlife Fund and the Marine Research Station.'

Corrie's heart lifted with the knowledge that Blake hadn't kept the money. 'Thank you,' she said quietly.

'I thought it was fair. The copyright will return to you in a month. Paul will be sending you the relevant documents next week.'

She nodded, unable to agree or disagree, hurt by the dispassionate tones of Blake's voice. A thought niggled her. 'Isn't it likely a burglar would be more interested in the yacht? Shouldn't you be there?'

'They don't know where it is,' he reminded her. 'But three of the crew are on their way to Sea Cottage. They'll take it in turn to do guard duty, although the yacht is monitored electronically. It's safe enough, I believe. If not, it can be rebuilt. Small boys can't.'

Corrie winced at his brutal words.

'Corrie, I'll ring the radio station and tell them what is happening. I'll ask them to make a news item mentioning that the photos have already been sold and despatched. It should stop any further attempts.'

'Everyone will know the yacht was the one in my photo,' she warned.

'That's no longer the first priority.' He picked up the telephone. The police arrived while he was talking and Corrie led them to her studio. She left them to it and went and sat by the sleeping boys, gaining comfort just by being with them. The day had been too long; Blake had ripped and torn her emotions into tatters, her studio had been violated, her work thrown around like confetti, but the threat she had brought to the boys had been the final blow.

The echo of male laughter and murmur of departing voices told her the police were leaving. One of the boys tossed in his sleep and she smoothed his sheet and blankets back into place, gathering love before going downstairs. Blake was locking up. She felt his glance encompass her.

'Go to bed, Corrie, you're exhausted.'

It was a quiet statement and she made no attempt to deny it.

'I'll make up the bed in the guestroom for you,' she said, 'then I'll start picking up the photographs.'

'Don't bother about the bed, I'll just put my sleeping bag on top of the couch. As for the photographs, they won't fall any further. Leave them. You can sleep easily, the police are going to patrol our side road until midday tomorrow.'

'That's good. There's tea there and plenty of food. Help yourself.'

She hesitated, wanting to thank him for his concern, but she was afraid that if she acknowledged her fears she would break down—she wasn't in the mood for making gracious speeches.

'I'll say goodnight.' She turned and went back upstairs, conscious of Blake's sombre gaze.

Sunlight striking her face and pillow in bands of orange, red and yellow woke Corrie and she lay quiescent, enjoying the play of colour until her thoughts remembered Blake's promise of love. Her eyes went to the clock on the bedside cabinet and she sat up, fully alert, wondering why she hadn't been woken by the boys. The smell and sizzle of food cooking and the sound of their voices followed by Blake's deeper tones reassured her, but she felt reluctant to get up and face Blake.

'Surprise! Breakfast in bed!'

'Look, Corrie it's us! We found Blake! He lives at Sea Cottage!'

James, Matthew and two black kittens launched themselves at her and she cuddled them, half winded by their enthusiastic arrival. Blake put the tray on to the table, unceremoniously scooped and dumped the boys and the kittens on to the end of the bed and then gave her the tray.

'All yours, the boys have eaten.' His voice was machine-gun crisp.

'Thank you.' She froze at the chill in his dark eyes.

'Blake! Blake! We'll come with you!' Two little boys were scrambling off the bed, their faces reminding her of adoring puppies.

'Sorry, I've got a few important things happening today. Tell your dad and mum to bring you to see me. I wrote my telephone number on the pad, in case you need it,' he added curtly.

Corrie felt his glance appraise her and was conscious of her peach silk nightgown with its soft cream lace.

'Peaches and cream! Pity there was a bug in the core. Goodbye.'

He went back downstairs, and Corrie heard the door slam after him. The boys moved to inspect her plate of peaches, loudly insistent on being shown the grub. They eventually gave her the plateful back after deciding that Blake must have squashed the grub in the kitchen. Her appetite had gone, but four pairs of eyes watched to make sure she ate everything down to the last crumb of toast.

* * *

'Today Mum and Dad come home. They've been married a week,' James announced triumphantly, having checked off the days on his fingers. 'What time do you think they'll be home, Corrie?'

'About five,' she smiled. 'But we've only just had afternoon tea, so it will be two or three hours yet.'

'I wonder if Blake will go past in his yacht again. Do you think he'd mind if we walked along to see him?' Matthew asked as he dumped a bag of shells into the pinic basket.

'Sorry, Blake invited you with your parents,' Corrie told him.

'But we're so close. . .' His eyes glanced towards the rocks.

'Don't even think it, my fine young man!' Corrie was learning to anticipate them. On the beach the boys could amuse themselves, whether they were searching for shells or fragments of sea-horses, or racing each other along the sand, but the rocks were forbidden. 'I'm going to sit here and check through the property columns, but while I'm doing that why not see if you can build an aqueduct?'

She had their complete attention.

'What sort of a duck, Corrie?'

Laughing, she explained, and sketched the design on the newspaper. Her smile faded as the boys removed the page to reveal more pictures of Blake and the members of the crew. It seemed as if the paper, the television and the radio had carried little else but articles about Blake Hanley and *Taiaroa's Petrel*. She had not wanted to read the papers, but had been unable to resist. The new knowledge had not helped. Blake's determination was legendary, his strength and his weakness was in his desire to build and sail the best yacht possible. She turned to the classifieds and glanced

towards the twins. They were holding a lengthy, frequently voluble argument on the aqueduct, but solved
the problem when each decided to build his own.
Corrie kept checking on them from her study of the
Property Sell columns. She had intended to find a place
while caring for the boys, but after one attempt had
decided it was a task which had to wait until she was on
her own. She ringed a couple of advertisements and
absently reached for a banana from the picnic basket,
her hand straying instead to the shell bag.

A crab, hidden under one of the shells, nipped her
finger and clung on for agonising seconds. With a yelp,
Corrie rushed to the sea to bathe the stinging, painful
finger, shaking her hand to try to lower the pain-level.

An interested query from Matthew prompted her to
show him her inflamed finger with its purpling marks,
followed by a lecture on crabs and shells, his loving
sympathy being somewhat sourly received. She soaked
a tissue and wrapped it around the finger, then looked
along the beach for the second twin.

'Where's James?' she asked.

'He's gone to get a couple of sticks for his aqueduct.'
Matthew pronounced the word carefully, savouring it.

'No!' Corrie gasped, following the line of sight from
Matthew's outstretched arm. 'He's climbing the rocks!'

She began running, intelligence speeding her limbs
with the knowledge that James was heading towards
danger, a crumbling, weather-worn cinnamon crag
eroded underneath by the sea, his target a clump of
bleached sticks like whitened bones.

'James, stop!' she called.

He did not hear, and she watched as he took a
running jump from the black rock to land on the
adjacent red scoria and began walking towards his goal.

'Stop! Stop!'

Her frantic cries reached him and he turned round in surprise.

'It's OK, Corrie, I'll be back in a. . .'

His chirpy tone ended in a yell. A section of the arched rock he had been walking along seconds earlier broke off and crashed into the sea. Corrie saw the white-faced boy try to turn back.

'Stay still, don't move! I'm coming, James!' She hoped her shout was more confident than she felt as she turned to the twin who had followed her. 'Matthew, run home. Ring Blake—the number's on the pad—if he's not there, ring Jenny at the Wildlife Centre. Tell them to bring ropes and rescue gear. Run!'

As he ran off she was already moving, climbing up the familiar black rock, until she was on a level with the ashen-faced boy. A chasm of a few feet separated them, dashing Corrie's hope that he would be close enough to reach.

'James, we'll have you away from there soon. The red rock crumbles like sponge cake, so it's vitally important that you don't move.'

'I'm scared, Corrie.'

She didn't see any point in adding that she was terrified for him. 'I'm going to take off my jersey and my shirt and tie them together,' her smile was meant to reassure the child, 'then my jeans, until I have a clothing rope—see?' She ripped the shirt into strips, then tore her jeans by pulling them on to a sharp rock, repeating the process several times before knotting the lengths into a rough rope and threading her belt through the last knot.

'Come and get me, Corrie!' Her intrepid adventurer had eyes of fear.

'We have to have the safety rope round you first.' Her weight could be enough to trigger the area of red rock, catapulting him into the sea. 'I'm going to throw you a line, but I don't want you to move to catch it. I want to see if I can drop it on to you, so you pretend you're a statue and stand very, very still until you can take it in your hands. It might take me several times to get it right, OK?' She said a silent prayer, then checked the knots. 'Once it's in your hands I want you to strap the belt tightly round you. Remember, don't move your feet!'

'I'll remember,' James promised.

It took her two attempts to drop the impromptu line to the boy, and she gave a sigh of relief as, knees rigid, he fastened the leather belt into position. She tried not to look down at the sea between them, the sea scum dirty piles of cream around the base of the rocks. 'Matthew should be at the farmhouse by now,' she encouraged.

'My legs are getting tired, Corrie. And your skin's turning blue and orange.'

'Blake would say I looked like a half-thawed chicken!' She saw James's nervous smile as she walked towards the point where the two rocks married, but she ran out of line after a few feet. By sacrificing her bra she was able to fasten one end around a point of rock. She crossed her arms to try to keep warm, missing her clothes despite the spring sunshine.

'Listen, James,' she said. 'We've got the safety line in place, if we hear any cracking noises then I want you to run as fast as you can and jump towards me. If I don't catch you the rope will hold you and I can pull you in like a fish. It's slippery on this edge,' she warned, 'so I have to stand behind this small ledge. Blake will be here soon with some rescue gear, but. . .' She didn't want to think how many minutes longer it would take anyone else to reach them. Shivering, she eyed the precipitous drop into the chasm which grew from the width of a hand to several metres as it opened to the sea. What if James baulked at jumping? She pushed away the thought. He hadn't worried over running along the narrow ledge to get his wretched sticks!

'Corrie, guess what! Your old binocular case is hanging halfway down your side. I wonder. . .'

She saw him lean forward, shifting his weight without thinking. An ominous crack sounded and small pieces of scoria began dropping. There was no more time!

'Run! James! Jump to me!' she shouted.

As he began running the rock groaned. The boy jumped and Corrie reached forward to catch him, both landing heavily. Behind them the scoria arch crashed into the sea, driving thousands of gallons of water skywards. As Corrie struggled to stand they were engulfed and she felt herself and the boy slip, carried by the downpour, both sliding on the slimy surface until the small barnacle-encrusted ledge gave her a foothold and the improvised rope attached to the rock jerked them to a stop.

'Corrie!'

Chilled and soaking, she wiped the salt water from her eyes. 'We're all right, James,' she reassured him, pushing the wet strands of hair back from her face. 'Let's just move slowly. We. . . Blake!' she gasped.

'Easy, Corrie. I'll take the boy. I'll be with you in a minute.' Blake picked the lad up, shouldered him and in a few quick moves deposited him on the beach. Corrie was reluctant to stand, her scratched and numbed fingers awkward, slow to undo the first hard-yanked knot of her bra. Chilled, she held the wet garments in front of her.

'You've given away the shirt off your back again?' His grin was a lightning flash. His arms went to the back of his neck and he yanked his own jersey off in a swift movement. He pulled the warm garment over her and she sighed with relief as he held her close. She knew he was just warming her as he had done once before, and for a moment she was content. It was enough to be in his arms, to feel his strength take over, to nestle against him.

'I'm all right now.' It was a wrench to move away, but she had remembered too much. 'The twins!' she said urgently.

He gestured to the beach. Both boys were dragging the picnic basket along the sand towards the path which led to the farmhouse. Blake bent and picked up a coiled rope and harness, and the sight made her tremble, her chilled hands catching at the knotted line.

'It's all right, Corrie, the twins are fine. Forget that wet rubbish! You need a hot shower.' His eyes contemplated her and his mouth curved into a smile. 'I won't even say a word about a thawed chicken! Let me help you.'

'No, I can manage.' She concentrated on clambering down, her body a soggy heap of shakes when she was safely on the sand. The knowledge that Blake was following steeled her to stand and look for the twins. They had gathered the umbrella and the chair, and the normality of Matthew's loud verbal assault on James reassured her.

'Healthy communication! Corrie, you and I could learn something!' Blake touched her shoulder, but she moved away, unable to contend with his gesture or the implied lecture. It was easier to deal with the boys. She caught them up outside the house.

'James, would you run and have a shower and afterwards put on your good clothes. . .?' she began.

'Go and take your own shower, I'll look after the

boys,' Blake intervened. Corrie opened her mouth to
protest, then closed it. One look told her he was not
prepared to argue.

The shower was gloriously warm on her chilled skin,
and with a crown of shampoo bubbles on her hair she
began to feel better. She sniffed the scent of the herbs,
appreciating their delicacy after the stink of the sea-
slime. Turning the taps on to full power, she let the
water massage her body, the steam fogging the room,
turning it into a sauna. Eventually, wrapped in the
cocoon of towels, she opened the window, guilty about
the time she was leaving Blake to mind the twins. A
short time later, dressed in a russet skirt and mohair
top, russet and cream scarves intertwined with her hair,
make-up applied with especial care, she surveyed her
reflection in the mirror. Sighing, she walked to the
bedroom door, setting her shoulders to face Blake
again as she went downstairs to the day-room.

'Corrie!' Boys and kittens ran up to her, engulfing
her with love. The contrast with Blake was as sharp as
a black and white graphic cut-out.

'I'm very sorry I went on to the rocks, Corrie.' A
showered and neatly clad James began his rehearsed
speech, then spoilt it by looking at his mentor, who
nodded encouragement. 'And I promise I won't go
near them until Dad or Mum, or you or Blake, are with
me to show me the way.'

Corrie smiled, 'That's a very good apology, James.'

'Blake says it's no good saying you're sorry if you
don't try to make it right. He says that's often the
difference between a big man and a little man.'

'He's right.' Corrie, sad-eyed, could not look at
Blake. 'But sometimes there isn't a chance to say, "I'm
sorry".'

James threw his arms around her to cheer her, his spontaneity heartening.

'OK, men—Matthew, your turn to shower and change and, James, I want you to tidy up your closet and the rest of your bedroom. I'll expect you back down here in twenty minutes, ready for inspection. Move!'

Blake's tone was quiet but effective. Corrie was abandoned as they ran to obey him even the kittens scampering towards the stairs. She needed to escape too. 'I'll check the casserole I put in the oven earlier,' she murmured.

'It's fine. We've done the vegetables, the table's set, the picnic gear's put away,' Blake told her.

'I'm grateful for your assistance,' said Corrie.

'Corrie, we need to talk, not make stiff little speeches!'

He prowled the room, his movements reminding her of a lean panther frustrated by his cage, but she was afraid if she comforted him she would be the one savaged. She had tried too many times to risk hurt again. Not wanting to meet his eyes, she leaned against the mantelpiece where she could look into the fire, flames gold, flickering orange with flares of midnight blue.

'Blake, I tried to talk to you before and you shut the door between us.' The words drifted away with the smoke. 'I knew you were hurt, and I wanted to help, but you didn't love me enough to let me.' The black log rolled, showering sparks, crystals of gold exploding as they formed. 'There's not much point in saying more, is there?'

'Corrie, look at me.' She felt his arms go round her and his fingers bit into the soft mohair. Reluctantly she turned to face him. The darkness in his eyes burnt like fire. A quiver trembled on her skin and Blake moved closer. 'Corrie, my darling, I'm so sorry. You made a mistake, but you tried to rectify it. I turned it into a betrayal of our love.'

Corrie felt his hands caress her, his voice a torment to her resolve.

'I'm sorry I wouldn't listen to your explanation. I wanted to hate you, it made the pain less. Paul tried to explain, but I refused to discuss it. When you gave away the rights to the photos I knew I'd been wrong, but I couldn't admit it. I was nursing my anger against you and against myself. The burglary made me realise the potential danger I'd caused you and the boys. I hardly closed my eyes all night, because when I did, your face, anguished and pale, haunted me. I wanted to charge up those stairs and make love to you, but I was too busy licking my wounds to see they were scratches which had healed.' He dropped a kiss on her hair. 'This afternoon when I saw the water engulf you, I thought I'd lost you. . .'

Corrie heard the choke of emotion in his voice. Unable to resist, she moved to comfort him, his need exposing her depth of love. She could feel his arms hold her, and his groan told of the wordless release of tension as she rested against him. He tilted her head back, his thumbs under her jaw, his strong, scarred fingers drawing circles of desire around the delicate line of her ears, scattering the thick curls that tendrilled around his fingertips.

'Darling, I love you. I don't deserve your understanding and forgiveness, but I need it. Without you I only exist.' He gave a tired smile that revealed the new, drawn lines on his face. 'That sounds soppy!' He raised his shoulders awkwardly. 'It's just the truth. I did try, but I can't destroy the love I have for you. I never

knew love was so powerful. If you ask it I'll give up the
race, the sea. . .'

Corrie reached up to him and gently brushed his lips
with hers. With incredulous hope flaring in his eyes he
kissed her with such tenderness and yearning that she
knew his hurt.

'Blake, the albatross soars across the oceans, sometimes with his partner but often flying free,' she said
softly. 'He couldn't exist on the life of a sparrow in the
cities or even a hawk in the mountains. I don't want to
change you or entrap you. I love you.'

'Darling, no wonder I fell in love with you!' He
kissed her with tender joy, the kiss deepening as their
passion and need for each other removed the shadows
of the past days.

He released her to look into her shining eyes. 'You
let me free, so I'm trusting you in the wilds with your
photography, Corrie. I'd like to keep you in Rapunzel's
tower, but you're an artist, and unless you carry on
with your career you couldn't be happy. And I want
your happiness, my little stormy petrel.' He bent and
touched her mouth, releasing a thousand birds wheeling and gliding in the sky of her emotions. 'When we're
apart I'll carry you in my heart,' he smiled. 'With you,
I'm a romantic!'

Corrie leaned against him. 'With you, I'm complete,'
she smiled back.

Their kiss was long and passionate, then a feeling of
being watched made Corrie pause and look over
Blake's shoulder. Two shining-clean boys and two spiky
wet kittens stood observing.

'You kiss just like Mum and Dad,' James offered.

'Are you going to get married too?' asked Matthew.

Blake looked at Corrie. 'Do you remember, Corrie,
quoting The Owl and the Pussycat? "O let us be

married! too long we have tarried. . ."' He waited for her smile of assent and tightened his arms around her. '"They sailed away for a year and a day, to the land where the Bong-tree grows."' His smile danced in his dark eyes. 'Maybe you and I could do precisely that. Mind you, I'm not sure where the Bong-tree is, but perhaps we could look for it on the Campbell Islands, and if we don't find it there we'll try Fiji, Pitcairn and sail up to the Galapagos.'

'Oh, Blake, my dream!' Corrie was alight with joy until she remembered her commitments. Blake saw the furrowing of her brow.

'You don't want to, my sweet?'

'I've got work booked up for more than six months, I'm due in London in three months, then. . .'

'That's all right—I've got a race, remember? I'm due at Cowes in three months. Not that far from London. We'll have to work out our schedules. I think we'll probably find we can match them. After the race we'll come home to Sea Cottage and begin plans for our hunt for the Bong-tree. . .you'll have to learn to sail. . .'

The sound of Philip and Misty's car interrupted them. With excited yells two small boys followed by two black kittens rushed to the front porch. Adding to the excitement, two of the great birds flew low over the farmhouse.

In the firelit room Corrie and Blake, realising they were alone, drew together, Corrie saw only Blake and Blake only Corrie.

my VALENTINE 1992

Celebrate the most romantic day of the year with
MY VALENTINE 1992—a sexy new collection of four
romantic stories written by our famous Temptation
authors:

> GINA WILKENS
> KRISTINE ROLOFSON
> JOANN ROSS
> VICKI LEWIS THOMPSON

My Valentine 1992—an exquisite escape into a romantic
and sensuous world.

 Harlequin Books®

VAL-92

HARLEQUIN *Temptation*

Rebels & Rogues

All men are not created equal. Some are rough around the edges. Tough-minded but tenderhearted. Incredibly sexy. The tempting fulfillment of every woman's fantasy.

When it's time to fight for what they believe in, to win that special woman, our Rebels and Rogues are heroes at heart.

Josh: He swore never to play the hero . . . unless the price was right.

THE PRIVATE EYE by Jayne Ann Krentz.
Temptation #377, January 1992.

Matt: A hard man to forget . . . and an even harder man not to love.

THE HOOD by Carin Rafferty.
Temptation #381, February 1992.

At Temptation, 1992 is the Year of Rebels and Rogues. Look for twelve exciting stories about bold and courageous men, one each month. Don't miss upcoming books from your favorite authors, including Candace Schuler, JoAnn Ross and Janice Kaiser.

Available wherever Harlequin books are sold.   RR-1

HARLEQUIN
PROUDLY PRESENTS
A DAZZLING NEW CONCEPT IN ROMANCE FICTION

One small town—twelve terrific love stories

Welcome to Tyler, Wisconsin—a town full of people
you'll enjoy getting to know, memorable friends and
unforgettable lovers, and a long-buried secret that
lurks beneath its serene surface....

JOIN US FOR A YEAR IN THE LIFE OF TYLER

Each book set in Tyler is a self-contained love story;
together, the twelve novels stitch the fabric of a
community.

LOSE YOUR HEART TO TYLER!

The excitement begins in March 1992, with
WHIRLWIND, by Nancy Martin. When lively, brash
Liza Baron arrives home unexpectedly, she moves
into the old family lodge, where the silent and
mysterious Cliff Forrester has been living in seclusion
for years....

WATCH FOR ALL TWELVE BOOKS
OF THE TYLER SERIES
Available wherever Harlequin books are sold